DUMBSTRUCK

DUMBSTRUCK

Sara Pennypacker

drawings by Mary Jane Auch

Holiday House/New York

Library of Congress Cataloging-in-Publication Data
Pennypacker, Sara, 1951–
Dumbstruck / Sara Pennypacker : drawings by Mary Jane Auch. — 1st
ed.
p.   cm.
Summary: When ten-year-old Ivy's parents disappear on the darkest
night of the year, she tries to find them with the help of an orphan
and her eccentric Aunt Zilpa.
ISBN 0-8234-1123-0
[1. Orphans—Fiction.   2. Humorous stories.]   I. Auch, Mary Jane,
ill.   II. Title.
PZ7.P3856Du   1994
[Fic]—dc20   93-32415
CIP
AC

To my parents
S.P.

Contents

DUMBSTRUCK

Prologue

One day, many years ago, a man made his way down the face of Mount Everest, the highest mountain in the world, in a tremendous scrambling hurry. Despite his great speed, the man clutched a thick packet of papers to his chest with as much protective care as a mother might give her newborn child.

The man was a scientist. He had spent the past three years studying clouds at the summit and had made a startling discovery, the proof of which lay in the papers in the packet. What the scientist had discovered was this: Swirling above the clouds was a layer of *pure knowledge*—a sort of smart soup, or brain fog, which he had named the Know Zone. He had also discovered that the layer was thickest in the middle of moonless nights.

In his eagerness to relay this vital and stunning information to the International Bureau of Scientific Things, the man stopped at the first village he encountered to seek a telephone. The village was no more than a collection of huts. It clung improbably to the fearsome face of the mountain like a droplet of spittle on an old man's chin, but it did, in fact, have a telephone. Of course, in such a remote area of Tibet, the connection was perfectly rotten.

. . . *crackle crackle* . . . "there's a Know Zone layer surrounding the Earth, above the clouds!"

"Very good! An ozone layer! A layer of ozone!"

"No, no! A *Know Zone* layer, a . . ." *crackle crackle* . . .

"Excellent! An ozone layer! We'll get to work destroying it immediately! We'll shoot the blasted thing full of holes the size of Kansas; we're scientists after all! Aerosol spray cans, that's the ticket! Thank you so much!" *Click.*

Disappointed, the man stumbled back out of the phone booth and onto the dusty road. Just then, as Fate would have it (Fate being a notorious practical jokester and not much of a humanitarian), a decrepit bus was rumble-sputtering its way along the single road with a cargo of farmers and their crated chickens. What's more, a chicken that had somehow escaped its cage chose that exact time to roost upon the driver's face, momentarily blinding him.

The bus hit the scientist at precisely the right angle and velocity to send him careening off the side of the mountain like a well-whacked tennis ball. Because the farmers were all dozing, and the driver had a chicken on his face, the tragedy had no witnesses except for a passing yak, who immediately devoured the spilled scientific papers.

Sometimes a small unnoticed event like this, a forgotten freckle on the monstrous back of Time, can have tremendous and far-reaching effects farther on down the line. Then again, most of the time it ends up meaning absolutely nothing at all.

Chapter 1

Something Was Really Wrong

On the third Saturday morning in June, an otherwise lovely and unremarkable day, Ivy Greene awoke to a house that was unpleasantly silent.

"Mom? Dad?" she called, searching the house in her nightgown, not really worried, but mystified. "Where are you?"

She dressed and searched her mother's studio out back and her father's workshed and the yard and the garden as well, very thoroughly this time. She looked under chairs and beds and in closets and beneath shrubs. She found a soft green lump that may at one time have been a cookie, and the Scottie dog that had been missing for several years from the Monopoly set, but she did not find her parents.

Ivy had been left alone before; she was, after all, almost eleven. But her parents were the very good and responsible kind who had never gone without telling her where they were off to and when they would be back. They would also give her a list of at least a dozen Things Not to Do, such as set fire to the house, or phone strangers in Australia. Ivy tried to push away the feeling that Something Was Really Wrong, but it kept sneaking back in to nibble away quietly at her bones.

She thought back over everything that had happened the night before. It seemed to her that when something truly terrible was about to happen to a person, something like missing parents, that person deserved a bit of a warning. Nothing spectacular—an unexpected change in the weather would do, or perhaps an ominous chorus of dog howls, or even a cricket in the sugar bowl. But as far as Ivy could figure, she had awakened Saturday morning without even a dark dream to hint at what was to come.

Friday evening had been pleasant enough. Well, all right, not exactly *pleasant*. Ivy's sister, Myrtle, had been over for dinner with her new husband, Oswell, and the meal had ended in disaster. But as Myrtle was just a walking pot of poison, and the average human being would have emptied the bowl of creamed spinach onto her head *long* before Ivy did, it had certainly been a perfectly *normal* evening.

Frank Rabidoux had stopped by after dinner to see how her entry for the Fourth of July Bicycle Decorating Contest was coming along. The prize this year was a ride in a hot-air balloon over the town of Hollington.

"Don't even bother to enter the contest, Frank," Ivy had told him. "I already know I'm going to win. I have inside information about Commander Bimwhistle."

This was true. Commander Bimwhistle, the town's oldest living veteran, who always judged the contest, lived at the far end of Popple Bottom Road (the same road that Ivy lived on). As it was her class project to collect all the recyclable glass from the people in her neighborhood, Ivy could not help noticing that there were seven empty pint bottles of Old Busthead Rye Whiskey beside his trash barrel each week.

He must really like Old Busthead Rye Whiskey, Ivy reasoned (correctly). He must like it so much, Ivy reasoned further, that he'd be sure to *love* a bicycle decorated with Old Busthead Rye Whiskey bottles! And so for several months Ivy had been collecting the empty bottles instead of taking them to the recycling center. She now had almost one hundred of them, all carefully strung together on long streamers of red, white, and blue ribbons. When she tied these onto her bike and rode around very slowly so they would not break, they spread out into a spectacular fanlike tail that made a lovely tinkling sound. Frank Rabidoux had inspected the rig thoughtfully.

"No one else has a chance," he agreed, clearly impressed.

"The prize is a ride for two, Frank. You can come with me if you want."

"If I haven't turned into a goat," Frank said miserably, sinking onto the front porch step.

Ivy sat down beside her friend. "Has it grown anymore today?"

"I can't tell; you look." He showed Ivy the little bump on his head that he hoped was just another wart, but that he feared might be the beginning of a goat horn. "I'm almost positive my toenails are growing thicker, too."

A few days before, Frank Rabidoux had very bravely, if foolishly, cut across Gibbie the Goat Lady's back field on a dare. For years, the possibility that Gibbie was actually a witch, and her goats were really children who had crossed her, had been the topic of heated discussions among the children of Hollington. Certainly Gibbie the

Goat Lady was odd, and she did indeed live in a shack at the edge of town with a great many goats and a great many cats. And you couldn't possibly argue with the obvious fact that some of the cats were black. And it was perfectly true that she always wore long, witchy, black dresses, and she was horrendously, murderously, scare-a-blind-man ugly.

Ivy was fairly sure that there were no such things as real witches, but she had read enough newspaper headlines in the supermarket checkout lines to know that stranger things popped up all the time. And those toenails of Frank's did look a little thicker. Ivy had vowed to help him find out, once and for all, if Gibbie was a witch. After all, Frank had been her best friend since the first day of second grade, which Ivy still thought of with mortification as The Day of the Hammerhead.

On that day, Miss Petherbuns had cruised the class as they drew pictures for an undersea bulletin board. She had stopped behind Ivy's desk, clapped her hands together three times very quickly, and announced, "Class, please make a circle around Ivy Greene's desk. She's drawn a splendid picture of a hammerhead shark, really quite a remarkable likeness, and I'm sure she'd like to share it with us all."

This had surprised Ivy, as it was actually a submarine being eaten by a bloodthirsty octopus that she had been working on. But when she looked down, sure enough, there was a hammerhead shark.

On the one hand, Ivy was extremely pleased that she had drawn such a marvelous hammerhead shark—who wouldn't be? But on the other hand, there were now *twenty-seven people ringing her desk and looking at her paper!* Ivy's lips were the unfortunate prisoners of war in this battle of completely opposite feelings; they were suddenly paralyzed and useless. A long thin line of drool fell undetected and unstopped from her mouth, and hung shimmering in the morning sunshine for all the class to see, just an inch above the remarkable hammerhead, before landing precisely between its eyes.

As Ivy walked home that afternoon, wondering miserably how she could convince her parents to move immediately to another continent, a short freckled boy from her class fell in step beside her. He did not make any of the hundred or so comments about the drool that he had a perfect right to make, but instead walked silently beside her for half a mile. Finally he spoke.

"We could make a gum-wad ball."

For three years they had scoured sidewalks and

bus stations together, and scraped the undersides of park benches and restaurant booths. The gum-wad ball was now a handsome specimen, nearly eleven inches across, and the friendship had grown into a fine thing as well. Ivy would not let her friend down now.

"I'll start working on a plan tonight to find out if Gibbie is a witch, I promise. And Frank, you can still come with me on the balloon, even if you are a goat."

Frank had left, and Ivy had headed in for the night.

Ivy remembered that she had not gone right to sleep, but had stayed up very late in bed, surveying the summer ahead. It stretched out like an enormous carpet, woven with innumerable possibilities, so vast that she could not even see its Septembery fringe. School had just let out for the summer. This was a convenient thing, as Ivy's head was full of a great many plans, and not a single one of them involved spending a day behind a school desk choking on chalk dust and multiplication tables. In addition to the Bicycle Decorating Contest and her promise to help Frank, Ivy had devised several ingenious plans to make herself fabulously wealthy. Most of these involved finding hidden bank robbers' loot, and quite a few were horribly dangerous, and one or two may even have been completely against the law. Ivy intended to get to work on them right away.

And then, of course, her head was quite boggled with plans for spending the vast amounts of money she would soon have: Army surplus night-vision goggles, an official world-class bobsledding outfit, The Amazing Luigi's At-Home Magician's Course, a banana rocket pop from the ice cream man every day. . . . So it was no wonder that the hands of her little bedside clock were tickling midnight before Ivy felt even the slightest bit sleepy. It was exactly then, Ivy remembered, that she had heard two voices, her mother's and her father's, drifting up on the soft June night air from the garden below her window.

Ivy poured herself a bowl of cereal and carried it out to the porch. She tried to recall exactly what her parents had said the night before, in case their conversation contained any clues to their disappearance.

"Velma, come quickly, I've done it!" she had heard her father cry. "The night-blooming stenchweed is in flower at last. This is simply phenomenal! There are only two vines left in the world, you know, and they haven't flowered in thirty-seven years!"

"Boyd, it's pitch-black out here!" her mother

had answered. "The night's so thick I'll have to slice it open with a knife to get through! I've never seen it so dark out before; there isn't a scrap of moon or a single blessed star in the sky."

"But that's exactly the point!" continued Ivy's father, growing very excited. "The night-blooming stenchweed is facing extinction because it needs total darkness to flower, and there isn't a single spot left on earth where the lights of some blasted shopping center or neon billboard or Styrofoam plastics factory don't foggle up the whole deal! Civilization's a plague, Velma, haven't I always said that? Inventing electricity was the single worst idea in the world, although tofu burgers run a close second. I'm going to write a paper on it, not that it'll do any good. . . ."

Ivy's father was a botanist, and it was his job to go hunting all over the world for the last remaining plants of species that were threatened with extinction. This was a very important job, and he enjoyed it quite a lot. But it was here in his garden that he was happiest.

Here was where he planted a few seeds from rare plants, and nurtured them, and experimented with ways to make them thrive again, and composed dreadful poems about them. And because he was so very happy, it was here that he did his finest, most inspired grumbling. Ivy's mother was a painter, and it was here among the eggplants and lupines and such that she did her finest, most inspired painting. There was nothing unusual in their being out there, even so late at night. All in all, Ivy thought that they were marvelous parents, and she shared their opinion that the garden was a marvelous place.

Flowers and vines and bushes and trees grew in a cheerful and untidy jumble from any spot of earth that did not actually stand up and kick them out. The garden was fringed with exactly the right amount of weeds. Neither so many as to say "a pack of hopeless slobs lives here," nor so few as to imply (even worse) that its owners were crazed with neatness. Just enough to announce to anyone with half an eye that the people who lived beyond this garden led such exciting and full lives that they had neither the time nor the inclination to attend to every weed. A family, no doubt, of sought-after party guests and enjoyers of limericks.

And, indeed, that was a very good description of the Greene household, now that Ivy's older sister, Myrtle, had gotten married and was no longer a part of it.

Ivy tried to remember if her parents had said anything else. She knew she had heard the village clock strike midnight, and had realized then that she was beginning to feel very sleepy. So sleepy that perhaps she did not quite catch what was said next in the garden below. It *sounded* like her mother had said, "Boyd, are you vacuuming my hair?" and her father had replied, "Why, no, dear, but I certainly will if you like," but of course that was ridiculous, and while her parents were quite often silly, they were rarely ridiculous.

At five minutes past midnight, Ivy finally closed her eyes, comforted by the familiar if baffling sounds of her parents below. She was delighted with the plump and juicy promises of the summer ahead, and absolutely tickled to distraction at the thought of her newly married sister living almost three miles away. For the first time in her ten and a half years, Ivy thought, as she fell asleep, as if everything in her world seemed just perfect.

She knew now that she could not have been more wrong.

Chapter 2

Tomato Feet

The morning crept by, slow and foreboding, like a rattlesnake crossing a warm rock. Ivy's parents did not return, and the bone-nibbling bad feeling did not leave. Ivy tried to take her mind off it.

She played a tape of Romanian polkas and sang along very loudly with her favorites as she went about her normal summer morning things. She laid raisins out on the porch railing for the catbirds, and spread the spines of lettuce from Friday night's salad out for the family of rabbits that lived beneath the little stand of raspberries. She opened the cover of the cold frame where the

newest of the seedlings were growing and gave
them a good watering.

Ivy returned the hose nozzle to its shelf in the
shed and her eyes fell upon the two oval red
loops of paint on her father's workbench. At age
six, Ivy had been suddenly and mysteriously inspired to paint her father's good leather shoes
red as a surprise.

It had certainly surprised him. But instead of
being angry, as a great many perfectly good fa-
thers might have been, he had accepted the shoes
graciously, had worn them proudly and often,
and had been moved to write one of his very
worst poems about them:

I've got mittens for my fingers, got a hanky for my nose,
Now my daughter thinks that I should have tomatoes
*   for my toes;*
They show up in darkest closets, and they make a lovely
*   squish,*
And they keep my feet from smellin' like a pile of rotten
*   fish;*
I'm the happiest of men, now, and my happiness just
*   grows,*
So I'm gonna wear these babies 'til they decompose!
Oh, there's nothing half as pleasin', no, there's nothing
*   near as neat,*
As reaching down and squeezin' my tomato feet!

Ivy's mother had brought out a pair of her best high heels.

"Paint these as well so that your father and I can have a matched set. You never know when we might want to enter a rhumba contest."

The faded rings of paint that had dripped down around the shoes brought a lump to Ivy's throat, and suddenly she missed her parents very much.

Now, Ivy was a sensible child. She knew perfectly well that worrying and growing lumps in her throat was not a bit useful. And so she decided to Do Something. She straightened her shoulders, marched back into her house, and sat down with a pencil and paper to make a list. Her list had three headings:

1. Why they might have gone away

2. Where they might be

3. Things I can do about it

After several moments nothing had appeared below these headings except a single drop of water, which may or may not have been a tear.

Chapter 3

Abandoned!

W_{ell}, if the morning had crept along, the afternoon was about to come hurtling by like a runaway train straight down the high speed express go-rails to Big Trouble.

Ivy had just made herself a cream-cheese-and-spaghetti sandwich, but she was unable to eat it because the lump in her throat was now the size of a honeydew melon. She was sitting on her stool examining the sandwich thoughtfully when she saw, out of the corner of her eye, a flowered steamroller plowing up her front walkway.

Pearletta Swicegood.

Ivy's father, had he been there, would have called out to her mother, "Velma, it's that *moron* again. How she ever manages to tie her shoes and make toast with a brain that small is beyond me. . . . I'm going out into the garden, Velma, and if you tell her I'm here I swear I'll come in and hose her down with the entire bottle of Slug-Be-Gone! I mean it, Velma, I *will not* listen to that featherbrain prattle on. . . ."

But, of course, her father was not there, and Ivy was left alone to deal with Pearletta Swicegood. And Pearletta's hat. At first glance, Ivy thought it looked like a goat's breakfast. On second glance, she was sure it looked like a goat's breakfast *inside* the goat. Ivy had to work very hard at not laughing out loud.

"Wait till you see what I've won today, duckies! *Yoooo-hoooo, hellooooo!* Oh, Ivy sweetie, there you are, go fetch your mum and dad, there's a dear. They simply must see what I've got right here, it is beyond belief. I simply cannot get over my astounding luck!"

Pearletta lived next door. Every morning of her life she plopped herself down in front of the television and watched a great many game shows, gobbling them up one right after the other like jellybeans. She had a positive mania for these shows. She'd go all hoopy, screaming out answers and guessing letters and spinning wheels and shaking dice right along with the contestants.

And then, every afternoon of her life, she would steam into town, in a great lather of excitement, and buy herself all of the marvelous prizes she imagined she had won that morning—all the skin-buffing systems and Whiz-o-Busy Blenders and patio furniture and Luxury Dream Caribbean Cruises the announcers had described.

Pearletta Swicegood had an enormous amount of money (it was her grandfather who had invented Molar-Busters, the world's most successful candy bar) and so this was not a problem. But she did *not* have an enormous amount of space, and so this *was* a problem.

Her house had long ago been filled to the rafters with golf carts and slipper socks and motorbikes and pedicure kits and washing machines and speedboats and microwave weed trimmers and E-Z Kitchen Waffle-Poppers and Croco-Hyde lounge recliners and electric mittens and solar-powered plate warmers and cases of Zippa Cola. Also her garage. And also the three large storage buildings she had had erected in her backyard. As soon as one building had been crammed full, Pearletta had simply locked it up and started filling the next.

Pearletta had recently purchased a large trailer and planted it on her last remaining patch of land. Already this was half full, and the Greenes worried that soon the vast ocean of prizes would begin to spill over into their own yard.

And still Pearletta kept watching her game shows, and still she kept buying herself prizes. And still she kept stopping in at Ivy's house to show off her newest treasures. And this was to turn out to be *very* unfortunate for Ivy.

"Ivy, where are your parents? I've just won the loveliest set of pearl earrings; they're so real they look positively false! No, no, that's not it, they're so false they look . . . never mind, you're just a child, you couldn't possibly understand. Do go run and get your folks before I simply pop right open!"

"They're not home just now, Miss Swicegood," Ivy said calmly, hoping that if Pearletta ever really did pop right open she would do it in her own kitchen.

"Whatever do you mean? Where are they? When will they be back?"

"I don't know, exactly, but I'm sure they'll be home soon."

"But that won't do *at all*, a mere child alone in a house! We'll have to get someone over here at once, you must be frightened half to death, you poor thing!"

And now here is where Ivy made a rather bad mistake. Here is where she opened up a very nasty bag of snakes indeed.

"Oh, no, really Miss Swicegood, it's all right, I've been alone all day."

"You *haven't!* You *mustn't!* You *never!*" sputtered Pearletta.

Pearletta stood gape-jawed as a haddock for several long moments, and then her mouth clapped shut. Her eyes began to burn very brightly and she seemed to puff right up like a bag of marshmallows in the microwave. Before Ivy knew what was happening, Pearletta Swicegood was on the phone to the Hollington Police Department, announcing to Chief Cliff Firmstone that she had "an abandoned child to report, do you hear me, an ABANDONED CHILD! Please send a squad car over to 41 Popple Bottom Road right away!"

And in only a few moments, a squad car came tearing up the driveway, sirens wailing and blue lights flashing, very nearly taking down a hedge of double white French lilacs in its tremendous hurry.

Police Chief Firmstone hopped out, looking especially bristly, and began to shout orders at the two officers who had followed him in a second cruiser. The two officers set to work charging

here and there, busily looking for clues and dust-
ing for fingerprints and writing notes in their
tiny blue notebooks. It was all very impressive,
and also quite overwhelming to Ivy, who, just
moments before, had been studying a cream-
cheese-and-spaghetti sandwich, and who had not
asked for any of this to happen.

Now, Police Chief Firmstone had had the mis-
fortune of being born with a great deal of shaggy
brown hair, a low forehead, and extraordinarily
long arms; all of which combined to make him
look quite a bit like a very large monkey. But, as
none of these features was his choice, you could
not hold his appearance against him. He was, in
fact, a fairly nice man. If you had to hold anything against him, it would have to be the fact
that he took his job very seriously. And as the
town of Hollington was noticeably lacking in any
kind of criminal activities, he tended to get quite
worked up and official on the least occasion.

Chief Firmstone began questioning Ivy in a
sharp, barking voice, as though somehow she
were responsible for misplacing her parents. Ivy
did her best to answer his questions, but when he
came to "And do you have any immediate rela-
tives living nearby, and I don't mean that crazy
aunt of yours," she hesitated.

"Well," she said finally, "there's my sister, Myrtle Pudge, over at Liberty Acres, but I really wish you wouldn't . . ."

Before she could finish, the chief leaped into action, ordering his two officers to rush off to Liberty Acres to fetch Mrs. Myrtle Pudge at once. Pearletta, meanwhile, left Ivy in Chief Firmstone's care and sailed away under her awful hat, anxious to attend to the unpacking of her various prizes.

Ivy sighed. Myrtle was lovely to look at, that much must be said in all fairness. Her hair hung down in richly waving sheets of reddish gold (Autumn Glow number 7, read the label on the bottle that stood above Myrtle's seat at the Hair's To You Beauty Shop) around a face as fair and sweet as a honeyed peach.

Ivy's hair, in contrast, was brown. Not brown with auburn highlights, not golden brown, not mahogany, or chestnut, or ebony. Simply, limply, brown. While all of the features on her face worked, thank goodness, and she had the proper number of eyes and such, everything had a slightly off-centered placement. It suggested that whoever had been in charge of arranging her face may have been new at the job.

Myrtle was fond of remarking that she had been given all the beauty in the family while poor Ivy had to settle for an overabundance of imagination, but Ivy was wise enough to know that she had been dealt the better hand in Life's little card game. For, sad to say, all of Myrtle's beauty could not hide a wormy and meanspirited soul.

Besides being terribly cruel, Myrtle was easily the most boring person Ivy had ever known, as she spent every waking moment attending to or discussing her great loveliness. And so it had been quite a relief to Ivy when, three weeks ago, Myrtle had left 41 Popple Bottom Road to marry pimply Oswell Pudge, who was easily the second most boring person Ivy had ever met.

The new Mrs. Pudge (Ivy thought this was a terrifically funny name for Myrtle to have ended up with) had set up housekeeping at Liberty Acres. This was the large housing development at the edge of town, where every front lawn lay as flat and even as a square of green felt, and every house was exactly the same as every other house, except for the dried wreath or the straw hat that adorned each colonial blue front door. Myrtle had not yet decided between the wreath and the hat, and this was a matter of great concern to her as she feared the whole thing might be some sort of test. She was very much afraid of making a mistake. However, she *had* decided that no weed would ever intrude upon her perfectly clipped green square of lawn, and that no speck of dirt would ever disturb the avocado-and-gold immaculateness of her new homestead.

The squad car came screaming and skidding back in a matter of moments. Evidently the two policemen had not given Myrtle any time to prepare herself, for she arrived looking like something from a bad day in another galaxy.

Her hair was clotted with an unsavory mixture of egg yolks, fish oil, and cottage cheese. An assortment of pins and curlers hung in wild disarray from the frothy yellow mass. (This was, Ivy knew, Myrtle's highly secret formula for Gloriously Swooshable Hair.) Tea bags were taped under her eyes (to reduce unsightly puffiness), and a ring of gluey green goop circled her mouth (for that troublesome oily spot). Her legs were smeared with a layer of hair remover thick enough to attract skiers, and around her shorts hung a strange contraption of candle wax, kidney beans and plastic wrap that she had purchased for a huge sum of money to melt away midriff flab. Great beauty was not without its price. There was a murderous look in Myrtle's eyes as the police chief explained the situation.

"And so you see, Mrs. Pudge, according to Article 17, Regulation D, you are now legally responsible for your younger sister here, until such

time as your parents return or she turns 18. I'm sure you'll be wanting to take the poor thing home with you now."

Myrtle's voice dripped with sweetness, and only Ivy heard the thin and dangerous crackle of rage beneath the sugar.

"I'm *dreadfully* sorry, officers, but there's been the *silliest* mix-up here. I'm not Myrtle Pudge *at all*, I'm only her *neighbor*. Just this morning Myrtle and her new husband, Oswell, left for a lovely cruise around the world, spur of the moment decision, you know, and they won't be back for . . . three years, no, wait, . . . four years, and I was only in the house to . . . to feed the cat! I certainly do wish I could be of more help!"

Myrtle turned to Ivy, and even beneath the gluey green goop and the tea bags her expression was clear: This was no time for Ivy to disagree with her sister. As a matter of fact, Ivy was delighted with Myrtle's invention, and thought it quite clever (and this surprised Ivy as Myrtle had never before shown any cleverness at anything besides hairdos and makeup tricks). As Ivy had absolutely no intention of going to live with her sister in the deadly neatness of Liberty Acres, she thought it best to say nothing at all. So the two police officers escorted Mrs. Myrtle Greene

Pudge-who-was-pretending-not-to-be-Mrs. Myrtle Greene Pudge back to where they had found her.

Ivy's relief was deep and joyful. It was also, unfortunately, short-lived.

Police Chief Firmstone's next words had much the same effect upon Ivy as a sledgehammer has upon a quail's egg.

"Well then, Ivy child, it's off to the orphanage for you!"

Chapter 4

The Wretched Dear Darlings' Blessed Haven Orphanage

Police Chief Firmstone assured Ivy as they drove to the Wretched Dear Darlings' Blessed Haven Orphanage that it was a perfectly splendid place.

"You've seen it, Ivy, as grand and fancy as a wedding cake, and I believe there's even a court-yard in the middle. And I daresay you've noticed the orphans out for their Sunday stroll."

The owners of the orphanage, Armilda and Borage Clott, met Ivy and the chief at the door, and Ivy sensed something horribly bad about them right away.

Armilda was as thin and sharp as a blackberry cane, and her hipbone left a deep and ugly bruise

34

on Ivy's arm when Ivy passed by on her way to the
parlor. A large, red, lipsticked smile curled above
a viciously pointed chin, but Ivy had lived with her
sister long enough to spot a paint job when she saw
one. Sure enough, the mouth at the center of the
full and curvy lips was small and tight and wicked.
That painted smile had fooled Chief Firmstone,
however, because when Armilda turned to fetch a
platter of lemon cookies, he bent over and whispered, "Sweet as your own mum!"

Borage Clott was as bulbous and pasty as his
wife was thin and sharp. His eyes, which were
located in a lizardly fashion near the sides of his
head, were the exact color and consistency of raw
clams, but everything else on the man was lumpy
and grayish. His skin was lumpy and grayish, his
hands were lumpy and grayish, and even his
teeth were lumpy and grayish. Not a single hair
grew from his lumpy and grayish scalp, but a
great many of them, bristly and black, poured
out of his lumpy and grayish nose. They rustled
about in the breeze of his breath, so that when
you first looked at his head you might easily con-
fuse it with a clump of old oatmeal in which a
large tarantula was struggling. A curious odor of
ripe cheese and toads hung about Borage Clott.

These two people seemed to have nothing at
all in common, save the fact that they both hated

children. Of this Ivy was quite certain, for adults who hate children cannot possibly hide this fact from them. Their nostrils will flare ever so slightly when they are near a child, as if they are smelling something dreadful, but are too polite to mention it. And there is something sharp and screechy in their voices (even when they are saying such things as "Hello, my darling, would you like a cookie?") that other adults cannot seem to hear.

Ivy could not imagine why these two people would want to run an orphanage when they so clearly despised children, but she would know the answer to this mystery very soon.

Chief Firmstone signed the forms admitting Ivy to the Wretched Dear Darlings' Blessed Haven Orphanage. Then he clapped Ivy on the back and told her she was a lucky girl indeed, and made his good-byes, leaving Ivy alone with the Clotts.

Armilda and Borage watched him walk down the brick path. The instant he drove away, they each let out a great hiss of relief. Armilda's long bony arm shot out like a whip to snatch the lemon cookie from Ivy's hand.

"Don't get too used to fancies, you little slug! And what are you still doing here? Get back with the others or I'll kick you there myself!"

Stunned, Ivy looked to Borage. He had removed his socks and shoes, and was hunkered down on the sofa gnawing on a lumpy and grayish toe. He took no notice at all of either Ivy or his wife, but chewed on the toe with ferocious intensity. The smell of toads and cheese was much stronger now.

Armilda took a sudden brutal swipe at Ivy, just grazing her cheek. Ivy fled through a door in the back of the parlor and found herself in a dark and shabby corridor. The corridor led to a long room that was even darker and shabbier, and covered with a layer of dirt that appeared old enough to interest archaeologists. In the room were a dozen ratty cots, and on the cots were eleven of the thinnest, most shadowy children Ivy had ever seen.

"Hello," said Ivy, to no response at all. "I'm not supposed to be here, there's been some sort of a mistake, and I'll be leaving in a few minutes if you'll just show me where the phone is."

The children looked at Ivy as though she had said, "I'll just be turning myself inside out now, and flying off to Neptune," but still they did not answer. Suddenly Ivy began to get really worried.

She tried to ask the children a few questions

about the orphanage, but they were all too exhausted to speak, except for one tiny dark-haired boy, the thinnest and most shadowy of all. Ivy sat down on the nasty cot beside him and began to learn about some of the horrors of life at the orphanage, enough of them, anyway, to discover that things at the Wretched Dear Darlings' Blessed Haven Orphanage were not *at all* as they appeared to the outside world.

The boy's name was Will. He was five years old, and so frail it seemed a pure wonder a puff of wind had never snapped him in two like a pretzel stick. He could not seem to speak above a whisper, and Ivy had to bend her head near his to hear him at all.

Will explained that the orphanage building was every bit as large and fine as it appeared from the street, but that most of the fifty or so rooms were the personal living quarters of Borage and Armilda Clott. The orphans lived in the four long and filthy rooms that formed a square around the squalid yard in the middle. The windows of those four rooms were small and high and barred and faced the inside of the square, so that it was impossible to escape or even call for help.

The children, and there were usually forty or fifty of them, worked all day for the Clotts at a

variety of jobs—chopping their wood or cleaning their rooms or washing and ironing their clothes or cooking their meals.

One of the girls near Ivy roused herself enough to ask a red-haired boy of about eight what had been prepared for the Clotts's dinner.

"Potatoes Lyonnaise was my job," the boy replied, "and I think Louisa made shrimp cocktail."

At this the girl brightened. "Then we'll have potato peelings and shrimp shells!"

At that moment Borage Clott opened the door and slid a large bucket into the room. Besides potato peelings and shrimp shells, Ivy could make out crusts of bread and asparagus ends and grapefruit rinds, but most of the food was an indistinguishable and horrid mass of leftover garbage. Ivy could not even consider eating from the revolting pail, but the other children seemed quite resigned to doing so.

"When I see you out walking on Sundays, everything seems perfectly fine. . . . I mean, I would never have guessed any of this . . . ," Ivy said to Will.

Will began to eat the seeds of a lemon, one by one, very slowly.

"Sunday," he whispered dreamily. "Oh, Sunday is wonderful. On Sunday we go outside! On

Sunday we sit down for a whole hour! Sunday is lovely; except for the sandpaper."

Ivy waited for him to explain. He nibbled a potato peel very delicately, as if it were precious, and then he continued.

"Every Sunday the Clotts dress us up and take us to church and walk us home through the park to show the people of Hollington how very well they care for us. Armilda scrapes our cheeks with sandpaper to make us all pink and rosy, and it stings terribly. Then Borage gives us each a whack on the backside to remind us of what will happen if we forget to smile, and that stings terribly, too.

"But then there's church, and for one whole hour we may sit perfectly still and not do a bit of work, and there's nothing the Clotts can do about it. And then we walk home, and that's the best of all, because we walk slowly and we see things! Like trees! Like sky! And families! On Sundays I see *families!*"

Ivy could not believe what she was hearing. "I see you every Sunday! You look so happy, and you always have those enormous lollipops, the very expensive kind that I'm never allowed to have!"

"Those? They're GLASS! They had glass lollipops made, with wooden sticks; we've had the same ones forever! And some of them have sharp edges, and some of them are chipped, and you have to pretend that they're very delicious and you are very happy *even if your tongue is bleeding!*"

"I don't think I want to hear anymore just now," said Ivy, suddenly feeling very near tears.

Most of the other children in the room had fallen asleep, still in their filthy rags, as soon as their wretched meal was over, and Will was beginning to nod his head.

Ivy laid down on the empty cot beside Will's. It was so narrow that her elbows hung over the sides unless she pressed them in very tightly to her body. The sheets were thin and gray and filthy, and there was no pillow. Darkness came quickly, because the few tiny windows dotting the top of the wall in the long room were so encrusted with grime that they would not let in even the most determined ray of starlight.

Thousands upon *thousands* upon *thousands* of spiders covered the ceiling above her, and they were crunching *thousands* upon *thousands* upon *thousands* of dead and crispy flies. Ivy could no longer see the spiders, but she could still hear them as they chewed their awful meals. She could not fall asleep for the dreadful crunching.

Several hours later, Ivy found herself still wide awake, unable to make sense of the strange and awful situation she had gotten into. She lay on her cot, trying to imagine what could have become of her parents, and then trying *not* to imagine what could have become of her parents, and listening to the gruesome sound of the spiders eating the flies, until she heard the village clock strike midnight. Exactly twenty-four hours had passed since she had heard her parents in the garden below her room: a lifetime and a world and a ten-minute police cruiser ride away.

Just then, from somewhere in the darkness very near her, came another sound. It was a soft whimpering, so quiet that Ivy knew it had to come from Will. He even whispered when he cried.

"What's wrong, Will?" she asked him softly.

No answer, just the quiet sobs.

Ivy knew that, of course, everything was wrong. This was a terrible place for a five-year-old boy to be: it was a terrible place for anyone to be. She thought of Will lying on his filthy cot, with no one to hold him or care for him, without even a pillow to catch his whispered tears. And then she remembered something.

Chapter 5

"Back to Sleep, Poopsie Duck"

Ivy got up and made her way out of the dark room and down the dark corridor, heading for the parlor at the front of the orphanage. In that parlor, which had so fooled Chief Firmstone and no doubt many other visitors, in that parlor the sofas and chairs were covered with pillows, Ivy remembered. The room was littered with pillows, clogged with the things, positively festooned with plump bundles of feather and foam. There were tiny satin pillows, nubby tapestry pillows, woolly pillows on the footstools, and even a dainty white eyelet pillow embroidered with the words Bless Our Loving Home. They lay scattered about as thick as fallen leaves in November, and any one of them would be perfect for Will to cry into.

Ivy found the door, and let herself into the parlor, which was bathed in the greenish light of the nearby Hollington Bean Processing Plant. She chose a fat pink pillow that was exactly the right size and softness. But just as she was about to creep back out the door, she noticed a pretty little quilt lying across the back of a love seat in the far corner of the room. She hesitated for a moment, and then decided to take the risk, as the Clotts were nowhere about, and were most likely upstairs fast asleep. She was very wrong.

As she picked up the quilt, Ivy heard the shuffle of feet on the front doorstep, and the click of a key in the door. She dove like a rabbit into the small wedge of space between the love seat and the wall, and held her breath.

It was Borage and Armilda, and they were in the middle of a really hot argument. Borage turned on the lights with a snort.

"Not Will! He's still small enough that I can tie him onto the chimney poker; I was counting on cleaning all the flues before winter."

"But that's exactly why it must be Will, you moron!" screeched Armilda. "The Botslovian Sewer Commissioner is looking for a child small enough to send through the pipes; apparently, they're having a severe infestation of rats. He'll be here tomorrow morning, and he's offering a thousand dollars!"

"That's not enough for the little maggot! We've spent a lot of money on him over the last five years." Borage crossed the room and sat heavily on the very love seat behind which Ivy was hiding.

"We haven't spent a thing on Will!" his wife countered.

"Oh, yes we have! Ten dollars, three years ago, for liniment and bandages at the vet's when the clod broke his leg."

"Oh, Borage, I'd forgotten!" said Armilda, her anger melting in her admiration. "How clever of you to tell the vet we had a pony at home for the little monsters that had sprained a foreleg! It's no wonder I married you, you are a brilliant little rum cake!"

Ivy heard Armilda leap up and plant a loud kiss somewhere on Borage's horrid head. She knew that people like the Clotts could never really love other people, because love can never sprout in mean soil, but she reasoned that they could probably feel a certain momentary fondness for anyone who shared their meanness. It must have been in this fondness that Armilda did such a surprising thing.

"But I'm afraid it really must be Will, he's the only one that will do. If I could, I'd save him for that rancid Dr. Smeedle who always comes in the fall, but this year she's being very particular. She's testing new methods of setting bones, and she wants an orphan with extraordinarily long arms and legs that can be broken in hundreds of places. That stinking twit Miles has shot up like a burdock weed this year, and he'll do nicely. And then she's asking for one with a great broad backside to use to practice giving needles all day. Seems grapefruit are getting too expensive. I've been feeding Leona a cup of lard every morning to fatten her up for that sale. Sorry, Borage, but I've got it all worked out, and it's got to be Will tomorrow."

"Oh, all right, all right," grumbled Borage, settling down deeper on the couch in defeat. His two shoes and then his greasy socks fell to the floor quite near Ivy, and she heard a low growling, slurping sound, like a dog gnawing a juicy bone. The odor of ripe cheese and toads that now percolated through the couch stuffing was enough to gag dead rats.

Ivy heard a sharp clattering, like meat knives falling into a drawer, and guessed that Armilda was settling her bony bottom onto a wooden chair.

"Now, let's see," Armilda mused, pulling a sheaf of papers out of a desk. "We'll have to invent an adoption for Will, in case the bothersome Child Services comes snooping around again. . . . I think it will be a lovely couple from Meadowmeade. . . . How about a Mr. and Mrs. Trueheart, no, no, I've used that already. Mr. and Mrs. Goodfolks, that's the ticket, a nice wholesome name. We'll make them both teachers, oh, that's rich! I'll give them two other loathsome little brats . . . twin girls. I'll name them Rebecca and Sarah, how revoltingly dear, to dote on their new little brother. It's all so perfectly lovely, I may *vomit!* How does that sound to you, Borage, my little poopsie duck? Borage?"

Armilda must be feeling that rare fond feeling again, Ivy thought. Probably thinking about the lovely thousand dollars she would soon have. But judging from the sounds now coming through the upholstery, either two pigs were slurping up some particularly wet slop on the love seat, or Borage-the-poopsie-duck was asleep and snoring. Armilda got up from the desk and crossed the room. (Ivy knew this because when Armilda walked, her leg bones made a sound exactly like rusty scissors slicing the air.)

"*Ooooh,* my little clam fritter is all tuckered out.

I'll just make you comfy right here. . . . Now where's that quilt?"

Ivy's heart froze in midthump.

Suddenly Armilda Clott's monstrously long sharp chin shot out like an ice pick over the top of the love seat, and rapped up hard against the wall. She swiveled her head until the bony plates of her skull knocked up against the wall, and her chin (which looked like it might have been used successfully to drill coconuts) tore into the stuffing of the love seat. Try as she might, Armilda could not manage a look-see into the tight space with that enormous and wicked chin attached to her face.

"Oh, well, it's June, I suppose you'll be warm enough. . . . Sweet dreams, you carbuncley bundle of bumps."

With that, Armilda turned out the lights and scissored her way out of the parlor. Ivy let out a deep and shaky breath.

The situation was grave, the need was urgent, and Ivy knew exactly what had to be done. She wriggled out from under the love seat and made her way down the filthy hall in a hurry.

"Will, Will, wake up! . . . You must, right now!"

Will sat up.

"You're in terrible danger, Will. They're going

to *sell* you in the morning. We've got to leave now; get your things!"

"I haven't any things," Will whispered.

"Never mind. Trust me. We have to escape right this minute."

"You can't escape, Ivy, it's impossible. All the doors and windows are electrified. If you touch them when the orphanage is locked, sirens go off and you get fried like a slice of bacon! Borage Clott wears the key to the orphanage door on a belt around his waist at every moment. You can't just go get it and walk out."

Ivy did not hesitate for one second.

"Oh, yes, we can, Will. That is exactly what we are going to do. Follow me."

Ivy grabbed Will, and pulled him down the dark corridor to the parlor. The boy's thin body began to shake like a china closet in a California earthquake when he saw Borage Clott lying on the love seat.

"It's all right, Will, just wait by the door."

Will did what he was told, although he looked at Ivy as though she were quite mad.

This was going to be a bit more difficult than Ivy had hoped. Borage Clott was lying on his side, and the keys were nowhere in sight. His lumpy and grayish stomach hung over the edge

of the love seat like a fifty pound bag of suet, quivering with every snore. Ivy gave a quick tug on his belt. The key ring was now just in sight, but it would take another tug to get the keys.

Suddenly Borage stopped snoring. He snorted and gulped, struggling to rise to the surface of whatever nasty dream swam behind the lumpy and grayish eyelids that now fluttered dangerously.

Desperate situations require desperate actions, Ivy told herself. Then she imitated the thin and slicey sounds of Armilda Clott talking.

"There, there, just a dream. Back to sleep, poopsie duck."

The revolting words worked like a lullaby on Borage, and he settled back into a deep sleep. Ivy yanked once more on the belt.

Quick as lightning, she unclasped the key ring and flew to the door. It opened with the third key, and she and Will were free.

Chapter 6

I-Told-You-So

Traveling with a five year old who had never walked free proved to be a very slow business. Will had also never (and Ivy found this just astonishing) seen night. The pale green glow from the bean factory was a pure and magnificent wonder. There was still no moon, but there were stars, and Will was positively paralyzed with delight that the sky should sparkle. A dozen times Ivy had to turn back only to find him standing with his arms outstretched and his head thrown back, drinking in the miraculous stars with his face.

Although Will would have been perfectly delirious just wandering around the sleeping town,

Ivy had a greater goal in mind, and so she kept hurrying the little boy along. Somehow, she had to reach the most sensible (now that her parents were missing) adult she knew. . . . Aunt Zilpa.

Aunt Zilpa was also by far the most interesting adult Ivy knew. She was a taxidermist by trade, and this by itself was a very interesting occupation. She kept a large freezer full of exotic animals ready to be stuffed, and she was fond of taking one out now and then for a practical joke. The minister's wife had once found a zebra in her shower, and a large baboon, maneuvered behind the wheel of Chief Firmstone's cruiser while he sat in the drugstore enjoying a second cup of coffee, had brought many giggles before it had begun to thaw.

Aunt Zilpa was extremely short and perfectly round, and there were many marvelous things about her. She believed that ice cream was a completely balanced meal, containing all the nutritional elements necessary for a long and healthy life. She had once impersonated a European duchess for six months, was fond of performing with the high wire acrobats when the circus came to town, and was enormously proud of the fact that she had never in her life worn a matching pair of socks. But by far the most marvelous thing about Aunt Zilpa was Pierre.

Pierre was an eight foot tall African ostrich: three hundred pounds of splendid bird flesh and feathers. Zilpa had found him as an abandoned egg while on a safari in the Sahara Desert. His name had come to her in a dream, and Zilpa was a wise enough woman to heed her dreams. Pierre was a vain and cantankerous beast, only happy when causing a sizeable commotion, and trouble clung to him like cheap perfume. In short, there was nothing good you could say about him without lying, except that being near Pierre was infinitely more fun than not being near Pierre.

And near Pierre and Aunt Zilpa was where Ivy was headed. The problem was how to get there.

Zilpa had left Hollington after an unfortunate mix-up involving Myrtle's wedding cake (which Zilpa had kindly agreed to store in her large freezer) and the rear half of a charging rhinoceros (which had been left in the freezer after she had stuffed and mounted the front half for the Hollington Hunting Lodge). The mix-up had caused quite a flap at Myrtle's wedding, and Zilpa had read the incident as a sign that she had been working too hard and needed a vacation. She announced that she was leaving for an extended stay in the tiny mountaintop town of Cheese Bend, where she intended to take up a rare form of thin-air yodeling she had long admired.

"Cheese Bend," Ivy told Will as they walked, "lies near the top of Mount Roquefort, which is just visible from Hollington on a clear day. Trouble is, it's at least a week's journey by foot. But the train makes regular stops in Cheese Bend; we're headed for the train station now." Ivy did not yet know how she would solve the problem of buying tickets without any money.

The night began to thin and lift. A woman jogged by, wagging a bottom that badly needed the exercise, and Ivy and Will had to hide behind a clump of laurel bushes until she had passed.

"We have to hurry, Will. I'm worried that the Clotts might have people out searching for us already."

This did not prove to be true, and the children arrived at the train station at dawn without any mishap.

Boarding the train turned out to be surprisingly simple.

Ivy found the conductor and explained to him politely that although she and her friend had no money, they would like to travel to Cheese Bend, where her aunt would gladly pay for the tickets. This seemed to Ivy to be perfectly sensible.

"Absolutely not!! Official Federal Rail Transportation Regulations!!" the conductor exploded, turning scarlet. "I've never heard such driveling nonsense! What you're talking about is a Delayed Purchase Authorization, and you'd need a Railway Form 15F with a certified signature and an attachment of Legal Fee Travel Waivers, which I sincerely doubt you have, young lady!"

The conductor pulled a very serious looking document from the center of his clipboard and thrust it at Ivy.

"*This*," he thundered, "this is what you'd need for the likes of what you're talking about! We're not just some amusement park ride here, missy, we're a class A, four-star, tri-scheduled, double-tracked, uni-national railroad company, you know! Now get along with you, I'm a very busy man! I have only twenty minutes to get to the dining car and eat my meal before I'll be needed to take tickets for the morning trip. I am not about to waste time on two foolish children trying to wangle a train ride, no, indeed!"

He turned crisply on his heel and hurried off to breakfast, not noticing that he left Ivy still holding the Delayed Purchase Authorization Railway Form 15F.

Nineteen minutes later, when the conductor emerged from the dining car, Ivy could see that he had indeed been a very busy man. And a very hungry one. Bits of fried egg lay drying on his

tie, a delicate trail of sticky bun crumbs encircled
his lips, and the unmistakable sheen of sausage
grease coated his fingertips. Marmalade crested
the waves of his hair like froth on a hurricane
sea.

"Excuse me, sir," Ivy said, again very politely,
approaching him to return the piece of paper.

The conductor took it, and began to puff up
importantly with the warm glow of I-told-you-so
too often seen on people who wear special hats to
work.

"There! What did I tell you?" he said to Ivy in
triumph. "This is *exactly* what I said you would
need! Did I or did I not say that you would need
this, little girl?" A single golden drop of maple
syrup hung from the conductor's nose and shook
violently with his impassioned speech, but did not
fall.

"Oh, yes, sir," said Ivy. "But I don't understand . . ."

"*Course* you don't! *Extremely* complicated! Why,
it took me years of conductor school; top third of
my class, I don't mind telling you! Now, then,
let's see . . . ah, yes, it's all clearly spelled out here,
very clearly indeed. . . . You're to have a first class
sleeping compartment with full dining car privi-
leges, and payment is due . . . this is a little harder
to read . . . in the year 2037; bit unusual, I must

say. Nevertheless. Train leaves in 10 minutes, best find your cabin. Dining car's third from the last; I can personally recommend the boysenberry pancakes, they're excellent this morning."

The boysenberry pancakes *were* excellent, as were the cheese omelets and the sausages and the corn muffins and the sugared doughnuts that the famished children ordered. The enormous breakfast took them over an hour to finish, as Will had never before had food that hadn't come out of a garbage pail, and he nearly swooned in rapturous delight over every bite. They were well away from Hollington by the time they staggered, round-bellied, to their sleeping compartment.

Chapter 7

"Borkx!"

Apumpkin-shaped wo-
man hung by her knees from a sturdy branch
midway up a fine specimen of a red maple tree,
in the center of the Cheese Bend town square. At
the first distant glance, she looked like an enormous, riotously colored apple. Brilliant bits of
odd cloth fluttered quite beautifully about the
woman's perfect roundness. Her face was an attractive shade of scarlet, and her hair, which had
been white since birth, spilled to the ground like
a waterfall of liquid silver. In her hands she held
a slim book entitled (although Ivy was still too far
away to read this, and besides, it was upside
down), *Famous Yodelers of the Last Three Million*

Years. It was the most wonderful sight Ivy had ever seen.

"Aunt Zilpa!!!" Ivy cried, running across the grass, pulling Will along after her.

Despite her great surprise, Zilpa vaulted neatly from the tree in an impressive double-gainer somersault, and swept Ivy into a hug that smelled unmistakably of Peppermint Swirl.

"You marvelous child! How did you know I was ravenous for you? I dreamt of you last night, a very ugly and worrisome dream actually, I was surprised you'd let yourself be in it . . . all about toads and cheese and vacuuming hair and pillows! Never mind. Let me guess: you're here to tell me that Myrtle has forgiven me for that silly mix-up about the wedding cake. No, that can't be it, your sister is a twit and a stinker. I'm sorry to have to say that, Ivy dear, but it's true, and there's no way a twit and a stinker can ever *stop being* a twit and a stinker, so I don't suppose she'll ever forgive me. But it really was a *little* bit funny when Oswell went to cut the cake, didn't you think?"

Ivy *had* thought it was a little bit funny, in fact she had thought it was the best part of the whole wedding, but she had more urgent things to discuss. Right then and there, in the Cheese Bend town square, she told her aunt everything that had happened since she had awakened to an empty house Saturday morning.

Zilpa loved her favorite brother, Boyd, and she was very fond of Ivy's mother, Velma, but she did not seem worried at all.

"At least we know they're perfectly safe, Ivy. If they had been in any danger at all I'd have dreamt about them, and they haven't popped up in weeks."

Ivy felt a great rush of relief, for what her aunt said was true. Zilpa set great store in her dreams, and her dreams, in return, treated her very well, never failing to alert her to imminent dangers.

"Just to be sure, I'll try to dream about them tonight. Now, you and your friend must follow me upstairs to my apartment and tell me everything about Hollington. Pierre has been in the most miserable sulk all day since I caught him cheating at solitaire, and you two are just the thing to percolate him out of it!"

Ivy trotted after Zilpa, feeling safe and hopeful for the first time in two days, and Will trotted after Ivy looking as if he were feeling safe and hopeful for the first time in his entire life.

Zilpa had rented a room above the Kozy Korner Kafe in the center of town. "The restaurant is owned by Bubba and Dottie Dobbelina, a middle-aged couple without children," she explained to Ivy and Will. "They had desperately wanted children, but none appeared, and this was a shame, as the Dobbelinas are very kind and would make splendid parents. Dottie is certain that their childlessness is due to Bubba's having been born during a total eclipse of the sun, while Bubba fears the cause has something to do with Dottie's weakness for pickled eggs, but neither has the heart to mention these suspicions to the other.

"Whatever the cause," Zilpa went on, "the result of their not having children is that Bubba and Dottie have turned all their parental hankerings and energy to their restaurant. The Kozy Korner Kafe (Dottie was firm about this name, although I hear Bubba favored the simpler Bubba's Grub) is the center of their lives, and they do a fine job of running it.

"Over the years, they have both become accomplished chefs: Dottie can make the most savory soups and casseroles, while Bubba's specialty is exquisite bakery confections. Because of their expertise, there isn't a single person in the town of Cheese Bend who doesn't eat at least one meal a day at the Kafe, and there are a great many who eat all three meals there with regularity. There are even those in town who, when the cobwebs have grown thick upon their own stoves, simply close up their kitchens for lack of use.

"It's the perfect place for me," continued Aunt Zilpa as she led Ivy and Will into the storeroom above the restaurant. "I just tumble downstairs for my breakfast (one of Bubba's excellent Bavarian blintzes and a generous dish of Rocky Road is my usual), and then I head out the door with Pierre and up to the top of Mount Roquefort for a lovely day of yodeling practice."

Ivy noticed that her aunt's room was large and open. Zilpa had cleverly arranged a variety of sacks and crates and barrels from the restaurant below to serve as tables and chairs. Several hammocks hung from the rafters like giant spiderwebs.

A large Canadian elk, which Zilpa had always considered her masterpiece of taxidermy and an indispensable traveling companion, filled one corner of the room. A line of freshly washed laundry hung from its antlers, a basket of chocolate mints from its tail. Zilpa leaped up and landed neatly upon the stuffed elk's rump, leaning back with a contented sigh. She nodded toward a large and well-worn leather suitcase in the center of the room, strained to the bursting point at the sides, that appeared to be breathing.

"I'm afraid Pierre is still sulking," she said. "We'll just have to wait him out. Please sit down and we'll try to figure out what happened to your folks, Ivy."

Ivy climbed into a hammock, and Will sat down beside her on a barrel of Greek olives. The suitcase cleared its throat.

"Now, then," said Aunt Zilpa.

"Harrumph," said the suitcase.

"Go back to the beginning," said Aunt Zilpa.

"HARRUMPH!" said the suitcase.

"I want to hear everything this time," said Aunt Zilpa.

"HHHAAARRRRRRUUUMMMPPPHHH!!!" said the suitcase.

"How I love that bird," said Aunt Zilpa.

Ivy and Will watched as a single eight-inch toenail emerged and delicately unzipped the leather bag. After one proud, still moment, Pierre unfolded himself from inside: three hundred pounds of magnificent disdain, looking as dignified as an enormous feather duster on stilts could possibly look. How he managed to fit himself inside the suitcase was a feat that astonished Ivy: why he insisted upon doing it was a mystery.

Pierre fanned his feathers in a rousing flurry of black and white. He straightened his neck in a move calculated to catch the afternoon sunlight on his iridescent blue and pink skin. He pretended not to notice anyone. And then, in a Vesuvius-like eruption of hiss, roar, and belch, he uttered the commanding cry of the adult male ostrich: *"BORKX!"*

At this, Will shot off the olive barrel like a launched rocket, which, Ivy knew, was precisely what Pierre was hoping someone would do. Greatly pleased, the big bird snuck a small peek at the boy, and then he stopped dead in his ostrich tracks. Normally at this point Ivy had seen him treat his audience to his most staggering display of fully extended wingspan, but all seemed to be forgotten in the wonder of Will. Or, more precisely, the wonder of Will's belly button, which was visible below Will's raggedy, too-small shirt.

Heaving a sigh of immense relief, the ostrich gently removed a tiny cooked pea from under his left wing with his beak, then tucked it firmly into Will's navel, where it fit perfectly.

Chapter 8

A Fairly Harmless Habit

Will did not even dare to breathe, as though he feared the pea in his navel might explode if he moved an eyelash. Ivy hopped off the hammock and removed it, tossing it out an open window.

"You'll just love Pierre," she told Will, "once you get to know him better."

Will did not look like he wanted to know Pierre at all.

"Don't mind his little habit," continued Ivy, "he can't help himself, you see, it's his obsession. Round things. He's forever putting them in his cheek or under his wing and carrying them around until he's found just the right tucking-in

place to stash them. Zilpa had him analyzed once by a bird psychiatrist in Paris, who called it the most severe case of Classic Early Nest Disturbance Syndrome he'd ever seen, and there wasn't a single thing anyone in the world could do about it." Ivy could not conceal a certain amount of pride at this pronouncement.

She then went on to explain to Will that many years before, while on safari to deepest Africa, Zilpa had come upon a grapefruit-sized egg abandoned under a banyan tree with no nest in sight. She had tucked the egg under her arm, where it had hatched the next morning into the ugliest, most demanding creature she had ever encountered.

Love had bloomed at first sight between the two. How Pierre had come to be parted from his nest had remained a mystery, but the result of the tragedy had been immediately apparent: The ostrich felt an unshakable and abiding need to put round things in round places. On his very first day of life he had spent three hours trying to put Zilpa's nose into her ear, and the desire had not lessened with the passing years.

"He manages to stuff Aunt Zilpa down a manhole once a year, and hailstorms drive him berserk, but all in all it's a fairly harmless habit," explained Ivy.

"And you mean you still like him?" Will asked. "Even with his . . . obsession?"

Ivy thought for a moment. "Actually, we like him even more because of it. It makes him more . . . Pierre-ish."

"I have one, too, Ivy," Will whispered. "An obsession. A really bad one. I never told anyone about it before, but I think I could tell you. Laps."

Then he admitted to Ivy that when he was about three years old, he had been walking with the other orphans on their Sunday stroll and had passed a plump, elderly woman sitting alone on a park bench surrounded by squirrels. He had been seized at that moment by a ferocious and overwhelming urge to *sit upon that stranger's lap!* Not a day had passed since then that he had not been tormented by thoughts of sitting on laps, but he assured Ivy that he had never actually done such a bizarre, and probably illegal, thing.

"Oh, Will! Lap-sitting is a perfectly natural thing to do—it's wonderful, in fact. And so is Pierre. Please give him another chance."

Ivy led Will over to the corner of the room where the great ostrich was hunkered down with Zilpa, poring over the contents of a large wooden trunk.

"The taxidermy kit," she said. "Come on, I'll teach you how to play Eyeball Parade!"

The trunk had been Ivy's favorite place to play when she was very little. Indeed, it was a box full of miracles, containing such fascinating and delightful items as rubber tongues and brain embalming fluid and gizzard extractors and (most wondrous of all) hundreds upon hundreds of glass eyeballs! There was every variety of eyeball you could ever hope to slip into a teacher's coat pocket or hide in a bowl of mashed potatoes—Indian elephant eyeballs, iguana eyeballs, panther eyeballs, wild turkey eyeballs, and, largest of all eyeballs in the world, South Pacific octopus eyeballs—all painted in the most satisfying detail. Zilpa had always been wonderfully generous about letting Ivy borrow whatever she wanted. Besides being just plain, marvelously good fun, the eyeballs had come in quite useful at school, as you can well imagine. But perhaps they were most valuable in Ivy's ceaseless war with Myrtle.

Ivy had only to float one in her sister's bottle of eye makeup remover to reduce her to blithering hysteria for hours, convinced she had somehow removed her own eye, despite repeated trips to the mirror. The ability to reason was not among Myrtle's strong points. Nor was memory; and so this trick worked week after week.

And only last summer, Ivy had found an eyeball to be just the ticket after Myrtle was named a semifinalist in the Hollington Bean Queen Beauty Pageant. Myrtle had become particularly insufferable, insisting on being addressed as your majesty, Queen Myrtle, and practicing the speech she would give upon accepting the crown. When she got to the line ". . . and I only hope my great beauty can convince the poor and the sick and the starving to stop being so poor and so sick and so starving," Ivy had thought she might truly kill her sister. Don't do it! commanded the Voice of Sanity inside Ivy's head. Glue an eyeball onto her forehead while she's asleep, instead! it further advised.

And so Myrtle had awakened on the glorious morning of the beauty pageant to find that a third eye had grown in her head. She had keeled over in a dead faint at the dressing table, and had stayed in that state of comatose shock for three days. And it must be said that a more peaceful three days had never been enjoyed at 41 Popple Bottom Road.

And now the taxidermy kit was working its magic on Will. The Wretched Dear Darlings' Blessed Haven Orphanage was not exactly a place where a child would learn the fine art of playing, as it gave to the orphans neither time nor toys. But Will was showing a natural cleverness at the business of being silly, and even Pierre seemed impressed. After about an hour of much-needed nonsense Zilpa sat bolt upright (or as bolt upright as a perfectly round person can possibly sit).

"Time to eat," she announced.

Zilpa had been keeping a sensibly watchful eye on Pierre, no doubt because eyeballs were, after all, very round, but she glanced away for an instant as she maneuvered herself to her feet. Just enough time for the ostrich to tuck a particularly attractive rhinoceros eyeball into his left cheek. Although both Ivy and Will saw him do this, neither had the heart to give him away.

The little group started down to the restaurant dining room, but Will stopped suddenly by the door. A large chart on the wall, with columns of numbers and photographs of a beautiful glowing sphere, had obviously caught his eye.

"What is it?" he asked softly.

"Moon chart," replied Zilpa. "Phases and orbits, waxings and wanings, new moons and crescents, things like that. Very important to know what the moon's up to, don't you think? Although right now it's more important to think about which flavor ice cream to choose."

"What's the moon?" Will whispered.

"Erk," Aunt Zilpa gasped, steadying herself on the doorframe. *"Pfa?"*

Ivy could see that Will's question had melted the ice cream right out of Aunt Zilpa's head, and left her not only at a loss for words, but also at a loss for the voice to speak them had they returned. She was not surprised.

"Oh, Will! Aunt Zilpa loves the moon! It's beautiful, it hangs in the sky like a star, but huge! It glows, and it changes from round and full to slivery and pale. It's silver and it's gold and it's *magic!* And Zilpa loves it!

"In fact," Ivy continued, "there are only two things in the entire universe that Zilpa takes with absolute seriousness: ice cream and the moon. She times the important events and decisions of her life with its ellipse patterns and gravitational influences. The greatest moon astronomers, from Hipparchus and Copernicus to Galileo and Cassini, are her personal heroes. But she says she'll never forgive the scientists from NASA who ruined the moon's perfect beauty forever with Neil Armstrong's size eleven space boots on July 16, 1969. She knows everything about the moon; every fact and fable, and she can describe every crater and rill, every mountain and fault on its surface down to the tiniest speck of moon dust. And that's why she just can't imagine a child who doesn't know about the moon."

Then Ivy explained to her aunt what kind of a

place the orphanage was. And in her outrage Zilpa found her voice.

"To come between any child and the moon is worse than criminal; it is inhuman."

"It gets worse, I'm afraid," said Ivy. "He's never had ice cream."

Chapter 9

Cheese Benders

Seated in the restaurant, Zilpa tried to enlighten Will on the mysteries of the moon, but was interrupted by a young woman who floated up to the table wearing a blue satin gown spangled with thousands of shimmering sequins. Necklaces and bracelets drooled from this vision of loveliness as profusely as vines in the Hanging Gardens of Babylon. Her hair swirled up like piles of yellow frosting, and she had the most enormous lips Ivy had ever seen, looking at first glance as though she had two bun-length weiners strapped to her face.

"How big today, Florinda?" Zilpa asked her.

The young woman smiled, and her extraordi-

nary mouth slid open until it looked like the kind of place where Pierre might hide a watermelon.

"It's coming along nicely, I think, dear," said Zilpa after gravely studying the stupendous lips. "About nine and a half inches across, I should guess. Now, I believe we'd all like some ice cream."

Zilpa ordered mint chocolate chip for herself (she solved problems best on mint chocolate chip) and vanilla for Will. (Zilpa and Ivy agreed that if he were going to be introduced to the wonders of ice cream, he ought to begin at the beginning.) Pierre had rum raisin (Pierre did not actually *eat* ice cream, preferring flowers and anything electrical, but he did like to pack the raisins snugly up his nostrils) and Ivy had black raspberry (because she wanted to). When Florinda left for the kitchen with the order, Zilpa told the children her history.

"From the time she was three years old, Ethel Plapp knew that she was meant to become a television hostess. She had her name legally changed when she realized that Ethel was the sound of a sneeze caught in your nose, and Plapp was the sound of a spoonful of yogurt landing on a linoleum floor. But Florinda Van der Vonne, now *that* was the sound of a television hostess!"

Zilpa explained that Florinda plucked her eyebrows out, and painted them back on an inch higher up on her forehead to give her the permanently astonished expression worn by all the best television hostesses. She styled her hair with an industrial-strength vacuum cleaner and gold spray paint, and wore spangled gowns and full-dress jewelry every day of her life, because one never knew when a Hollywood talent agent might wander by. She worked as a waitress at the Kafe as it seemed the most likely place in town to be spotted. Besides, the job provided lipstick money and excellent practice in the skills she would need in Hollywood. But the greatest measure of her dedication to her dream was this: Each night she went to bed with the corners of her lips taped to her ears, to stretch them into a smile large enough to cause even the most canyon-mouthed of TV beauties to weep with jealousy.

"When Pierre looks at her mouth, I just know he's dreaming of basketballs!"

Over the ice cream, which caused Will to fall completely off his chair in a stupor of delirious pleasure, Zilpa began again to educate the boy on moon lore. But it wasn't long before both he and Ivy lost interest in the waxings of the gibbous moon, and began to study instead the far more fascinating customers of the Kozy Korner Kafe. As the dining room was a small and neighborly place, with its tables nuzzling one another like friendly puppies, Ivy noticed right away that the patrons were not the sort of people likely to win spots in a milk commercial. Zilpa gave up and educated them on the customers.

"Loel Hoober over there," she explained, "awakened on the morning of his sixteenth birthday (after having gone to bed the night before with chin skin as smooth as a buttered eel) to find his pillow in shreds, and his face skewered three inches into his mattress by a beard that was clearly something special.

"The thing grows at an alarming rate, and could reach the size of a Lincoln sedan in just a week if not trimmed with a band saw daily. But it doesn't cause him any real inconvenience, except in the matter of his meals. Loel has to feed himself through the dozens of tunnels that shoot through his astonishing beard. All of them lead eventually to his mouth, but he is never sure how long the trip will take. To compensate for this time-delay feature, which seems to average six hours, Loel simply orders his food one meal ahead—having his morning coffee and doughnuts the evening before, and his afternoon ham on rye when he awakens."

Florinda fluttered up to his table. "It's so *marvelous* to see you here, Loel!" she gushed into the eraser end of her pencil which she held like a microphone. "And what exciting and valuable dishes may I bring to you tonight?"

Loel stroked his beard thoughtfully before answering. "I believe I'll have a hankering for French toast and bacon tomorrow morning. Oh, and coffee. I'll probably want coffee."

Just then Ivy and Will were distracted by two elderly women who settled their considerable bulks into the booth on the other side of the Kafe, and heaved twin sighs of relief.

Mavis and Mona Grimble were cousins, but they shared a much stronger bond as well, Zilpa volunteered. They both collected illnesses the way other people collected stamps or butterflies, ever watchful for a rarer or more exotic variety, or an opportunity to show off a newly acquired specimen.

"Lovely people, really, but it's not wise to ask them how they are if you're in a hurry," confided Zilpa.

Mona glanced down at Mavis's feet as she slid them under the booth.

"Mavis," she cried in utter astonishment, "your toes are lookin' fine!"

Mavis held up the toes in question, which protruded from her sandals like five plump sausages. Pierre eyed them for possible roundness.

"It's a marvel, I tell you, it's a gift from above that the bunions have finally fallen off. And to think that it happened at old Doc Bumbry's funeral service, of all places! Right in the middle of the cryingest part, off they popped into my stockin's like little cocktail onions! Have I told you this before, Mona?"

"Yes, yes, you have, Mavis, but I could hear it a thousand times. It reminds me of that time I had that boil burst on my neck, the size of a beefsteak tomato it was, *ruined* my new housedress. 'Course it wasn't just the one, no, it was a *plague* of boils that cursed me. And do you recall what a time I had when my spleen swelled up like a good cheese souffle? Well, it was touch and go there for the longest time. . . ."

Ivy and Will heard no more of popping bunions or bursting boils or swelling spleens, for at that moment Florinda appeared at the cousins' table to tell them that the special of the day was lamb stew, and to let them admire her lovely teeth and skin.

"I cannot eat lamb stew, dear, oh, it gasses me up somethin' terrible!" said Mavis, shaking her head sadly.

"Nor I, what with my liver bein' so skittish and all," agreed Mona.

And with many sympathetic clucks and shakes

of their heads, the cousins regretfully ordered dry toast and tea.

"How *awful*, dry toast and tea!" Ivy whispered to Aunt Zilpa.

"Not a bit. Those two could eat bullet casings and rat poison, and come back for seconds. Florinda knows to bring them the stew, lots of it, and then keep back a safe distance when they tuck in to it."

Sure enough, Florinda returned in a few moments to set two huge platters in front of the ailing cousins. Four elbows pumped like steam pistons in overdrive, and sparks flew from both forks. The sound produced was exactly that of a harbor dredge vacuuming up a particularly mucky stretch of sludge, and in a matter of seconds the platters had been scoured spotless and the women were tussling over the dessert menu.

"I couldn't possibly have dessert, my bile production being so delicately balanced, of course," said Mavis, emerging from the struggle with the menu.

"Well, it's out of the question for me. The doctor says I'm a gallbladder attack waiting to happen!" agreed Mona after she had wrestled it from her cousin's grip.

Ivy smiled. If she didn't have so much to worry about, she thought she might enjoy these Cheese

Bend-ers very much. She had always preferred people who were slightly or even seriously odd, to the ordinary, run-of-the-mill, meat-loaf-and-vanilla-pudding sort. After all, she thought, you wouldn't buy a pound of orange jelly beans if you could have a pound of assorted gourmet flavors. And the 128 crayons in the deluxe artist's box would not be nearly so deluxe if they were all one color. And Cheese Bend was definitely a variety pack kind of town.

Suddenly, a very large man, who was wearing what appeared to be an orange tornado on his head, burst through the kitchen door and rushed to the table. He was covered from wig to toe with raspberry jam.

"The doughnut-stuffer! It's gone all bonkers, and it's *attacking* me! Zilpa, you must come and take a look!"

In exchange for room and board, Zilpa kept the restaurant equipment in good working order, as she was a natural whiz with machines, and neither Bubba nor Dottie was. Zilpa followed Bubba and his atrocious wig, and Ivy and Will followed Zilpa. Pierre, who had wandered off to search the jukebox in vain for an ostrich-sized opening, saw the parade and joined in behind Will, hoping to get a glimpse of the kitchen. Pierre tried at every opportunity to pass through the swinging doors, sensing that the room behind contained unspeakable wonders, but Zilpa had wisely never allowed him in.

Today was his lucky day. Zilpa had immediately been hit smack in the eye with a gob of raspberry jam hurled from the misbehaving doughnut-stuffer, and because she was temporarily blinded, Pierre entered the kitchen unnoticed. What he saw inside struck him absolutely dumb with delight, so goggling him that he very nearly swallowed the glass rhinoceros eye. Giant silver machines of every description were toasting and roasting and chopping and tossing and blending and stuffing and frying and glazing in a heavenly frenzy. The doughnut-stuffer in the center of the room was lurching about like a rabid dog, spewing great gobs of sticky jam upon all within range, but to Pierre, this added immensely to the appeal.

He hurried over to try to intercept a blob but Ivy didn't think Aunt Zilpa was in a mood for nonsense.

"Stay out of the way until Aunt Zilpa's done here," she warned the ostrich. "And don't get into any trouble!"

Pierre dragged himself away with great slow sulking steps. But he forgot the injustice as soon as he spied the enormous Batter King mixer whizzing away in the corner, with its big-as-a-bathtub bowl full of mint pink batter.

The Dobbelinas were famous for their Cherry Marshmallow Cheesecake, which owed its remarkable smoothness to a full hour's beating in the Batter King. The whirling pink mixture crept up the sides of the bowl, leaving a funnel-shaped hole in the center that looked to Pierre as if it were *precisely* the dimensions of a rhinoceros eyeball. He quickly fired the eyeball out of his cheek and watched, satisfied, as it sank into its soft pink nest. The spinning batter hypnotized the ostrich, and he greatly enjoyed his growing dizziness. By the time Zilpa called to him, having fixed the doughnut-stuffer with a hairpin and some dental floss, his head was whirling and there seemed to be no clear connection between his legs and the rest of his body.

He took a step toward the center of the room and reeled instead into a rack of shelves laden with Greek salads and chocolate layer cakes. A mountain gorilla armed with a battering ram could not have done more damage. Pierre sat in the center of the mess, squishing fudge and feta cheese between his great toes, and sighed happily.

Bubba Dobbelina was exceptionally patient and kind, and he was very fond of Pierre, but he was also fond of his kitchen, and so he threw Pierre a look that could have melted zinc.

Ivy knew that Pierre had received this look before. It had been hurled at him by countless bank managers, grocery clerks, dentists, and theater ushers under pretty much the same circumstances, and so she thought it might be time to beat a hasty retreat. She dragged the ostrich, followed by Will and Zilpa, back out to the dining room where they ran into Bubba's wife, Dottie.

Dottie was as patient and kind as her husband (although she was a good deal shorter, and had much better hair) and she was in a better mood, as she had not seen the mess in the kitchen. She was delighted to meet Ivy and Will, and as she was the motherly sort, she noticed right away that they were both very tired. Especially Will, who could not stop yawning.

"He hasn't had much sleep," Ivy reminded her aunt.

"Let's go upstairs and fix him a hammock," agreed Aunt Zilpa.

"Wait," said Dottie. "I've got a better idea. Bubba and I have always kept a little room ready in case we should ever be blessed with a child. Doesn't seem as that's too likely tonight, so the boy's welcome to use it. It's just down the hall."

Ivy followed Will into his new room. It was

simple, but it contained everything a five year old would want, right down to a pair of clean pajamas. Will was wonder-struck.

"Pick out a story, and I'll read it to you," Dottie offered.

Will did not know what to choose, but Zilpa did.

"He's got to start somewhere," she said, handing *Goodnight, Moon* to Dottie.

Dottie settled herself on the rocking chair with the book.

"Why don't you come on over here, Will, and sit on my lap?"

Before she turned to head upstairs with Aunt Zilpa, Ivy gave Will a wink. The smile on Will's face was as wide as Florinda's.

Chapter 10

Mavis's Eyeball

The days slipped by one by one, not looking a bit like weeks to Ivy until they were stacked up well behind her. She could see that they were the most joyful Will had ever known.

The little boy proved to be a terrific help in all areas of the restaurant, and a natural cook.

"Another teaspoon of tarragon," he would recommend to Dottie after sniffing the soup of the day.

"More almond paste in the shortbread, I think," he would say to Bubba, to correct a crumbling torte. And he would be right.

Ivy watched Will grow plump on the very best

the restaurant had to offer, but she saw that he was truly nourished by the hugs and smiles and small kindnesses that fell upon him like sunshine. His voice grew stronger every day, and within a week he was singing and shouting, and even yodeling with Aunt Zilpa. Curiously enough, of all the joys and rights and duties of normal childhood that had been missing at the orphanage, mischief had been missed the most of all. Therefore, Will found Pierre's gift for causing trouble utterly delicious.

Ivy had to agree.

One day at breakfast, for example, Will and Ivy and Zilpa and Pierre were seated beside the Grimble cousins. Mavis had just polished off a wheelbarrow-sized order of the Belly-Stretcher Special, and was rounding out the meal with enough Cherry Marshmallow Cheesecake to feed Rhode Island, when she discovered an eyeball in her mouth. Ivy and Will recognized it as the one they had seen Pierre snatch from the taxidermy kit.

"Oh, my stars!" cried Mavis, spitting it out. "I've got Displaced Eyeball Syndrome, I've felt it coming for months! No, it's Eye-in-Mouth Disease! Call the doctor, alert the medical researchers!"

Pierre was studying his reflection intently in the chrome napkin holder.

Mona had seen the eyeball come out of her cousin's mouth, and was quite impressed, but she was not about to show it.

"Why that's *nothin'*, Mavis, it happens to me *all the time!* When your *brain* starts leakin' through, *that's* when you've got to worry. Have one of your pills, now, dearie, that'll settle you down, you don't want to be givin' yourself apoplexy like I did. Have I told you about my apoplexy? Well . . ."

But Mavis was not about to settle down, not with this marvelous new symptom. She leaped out of the booth and bounded over tables with an agility that would have been remarkable in a world-class hurdler, never mind an eighty-year-old woman with lumbago, bad knees, and the vapors.

The rest of the customers followed Mavis outside, where her hysteria seemed likely to reach a staggering peak. Florinda tried valiantly to hostess the event, and only Ivy and Will stayed behind to watch what Pierre would do next.

The ostrich headed straight through the unguarded kitchen door. Although his invasion was short (Bubba kicked him back out the door less

than ten seconds later), it was apparently successful: There was a significant bulge under his right
wing.

Ivy and Will followed Pierre as he sauntered
out of the restaurant to join the commotion on
the street, only pausing for the briefest, most in-
nocent second to snatch a meatball from Loel
Hoober's plate of spaghetti and tuck it under his
left wing.

Outside, Loel generously offered to transport
Mavis to the doctor in the back of his pickup
truck, and the rest of the breakfast patrons got
busy trying to secure the flailing woman and hoist
her up for the ride. Pierre appeared to be as
worried and helpful as any in the crowd at the
back end of the truck, and only Ivy and Will saw
him cram the meatball firmly up the exhaust
pipe. Pierre's eyes glazed over slightly, but otherwise he gave no indication of his accomplish-
ment.

The truck made it thirty feet down the road
before it seized and bucked, shooting poor Mavis
and her displaced eyeball up into the air in glorious defiance of the laws of gravity, across the
village green and directly into the duck pond.

The spectacle was watched in openmouthed
wonder, and, of course, no one was more open-

mouthed than Florinda. The situation proved too tempting for Pierre. From under his right wing he produced a large ball of bread dough and stuffed it into the waitress's cavernous mouth with a magician's lightness and speed. Florinda never knew what hit her, but Will did.

"Bubba's   Secret-Recipe-Mile-High-Marvel Loaf! We've got to get it out quickly!"

Too late. The dough rose with enthusiasm in the warmth of Florinda's mouth, but in a curious chemical reaction with her lipstick, hardened like Portland cement. Her freedom that afternoon required a jackhammer, a crowbar, and language that cannot be repeated here.

Poor Ivy. No matter how much trouble Pierre got into, she couldn't forget about the Wretched Dear Darlings' Blessed Haven Orphanage, where the children ate garbage and were sold to monstrous fates. And no matter how kind the Dobbelinas were, or how wonderful it was to be with Aunt Zilpa, the knowledge that her parents had vanished hung over Ivy like a dark moon in a bad dream.

Day after day, she and Zilpa would climb to the top of Mount Roquefort, where the yodeling was fine and where, curiously enough, Zilpa claimed her brain juice fizzed at a higher frequency.

"If we're ever going to figure this thing out,

we'll do it up here, Ivy. There's something in the air, something *smart*, I'm just sure of it. Did you know that only Mount Everest, in the Himalayas, is higher, and that the Tibetan monks who live up there are the wisest people on Earth?"

Ivy agreed that her thoughts were a lot clearer up above the clouds. In fact, she solved many complicated puzzles that had mystified her before, such as how she could find out if Gibbie the Goat Lady was a witch.

Sitting above the clouds one day, the answer had just fallen into her head: she could take Gibbie's picture. Everyone knows that witches don't show up on film, so she could hide in Gibbie's back field, disguised as a bush, and take her picture. The problem, of course, was that by now it wouldn't matter. For all she knew, Frank Rabidoux was butting horns with the other goats in Gibbie's field.

Sadly, for all the boost in brainpower Ivy and Zilpa felt up there on top of Mount Roquefort, they made no progress at all in the matter of her parents.

Once, however, Ivy had leaped off her ledge in midyodel, struck by a notion of startling brilliance. "It *was* darker than usual in the garden that night, my parents were right! And it wasn't just because there was no moon!"

Zilpa helped herself to another dish of butter pecan ice cream from the special insulated pack she always brought with her, and waited for Ivy to explain.

"The Bean Processing Plant . . . Oswell said it was closed that night!"

"Tell me what happened, and don't leave anything out," Zilpa encouraged.

"I'll try. Myrtle and Oswell had been over for dinner on the very night I heard my parents out in the garden. They had both had the day off from their jobs at the Hollington Bean Processing Plant because the plant was closed for its annual repairs to the gas venting pipe. Oswell is the Head Vent Pipe Engineer, and he said that during bean processing an enormous amount of explosive gas is produced that must be vented to avoid disaster. And that the pipe had to be cleaned once a year before the first crop came in. Oswell had bored us all stiff with his explanation of all this, and then Myrtle had bored us all dead rigid with her description of her new job. She's a bean counter now."

"Deadly stuff," Zilpa said sympathetically, licking her bowl clean. "It's a wonder you stayed awake through it all."

"She went on and on about how hard it must be for the other bean counters to work, what with the distraction of her great loveliness and all, and then she kept shaking her head sadly and saying, 'Great beauty can be such a curse sometimes, not that *Ivy* will ever know what I mean.' I held my temper as long as I could, I really did, Aunt Zilpa, but when she said it for the fifth time, I just couldn't help myself. I emptied the bowl of creamed spinach onto her head."

"Perfectly understandable, I've often been tempted to do exactly the same thing myself, dear," said Aunt Zilpa. "Please go on."

"Well, that pretty much ended the evening, but I remember now that when Myrtle and Oswell headed home it was darker than usual. And that must have been because it was the one night of the year that the Bean Processing Plant was closed down! Normally the machines run all night, and the glow from the factory lights up half the town."

Interesting as all this was, however, it brought them no closer to figuring out what might have happened to Ivy's parents. Before long, Ivy began to feel that she would have to return to Hollington if she were ever going to kiss their cheeks again, and the feeling grew stronger every day, despite Zilpa's objections.

"But what if they're there, waiting for me, needing me?"

"But what if you're caught, and sent back to the Clotts?"

"I'll ride Pierre, I'll go at night, I won't get caught."

And in the end Zilpa gave in, and Ivy set off for Hollington.

Chapter 11

Dumber than Soup

An ostrich can travel up to forty miles per hour, and even with Ivy on his back Pierre made good time. They rode through the night, accompanied only by a slivery moon, avoiding main streets and stopping just twice: once beside a mountain stream to pick up a fish that was bloated in death to the roundness of knockwurst, and then once more to deposit the fish in one of the black boots that stood upon Police Chief Firmstone's darkened front doorstep. They arrived at 41 Popple Bottom Road in the last few blue moments before dawn.

The newspaper carrier had continued to de-

liver the Greenes' *Hollington Daily Times*; the cop-
ies lay stacked and unread on the front porch
where they had yellowed and dampened only
slightly. The air inside the house was as still and
silent as stone, and the soft green mold that covered what had once been a cream-cheese-and-
spaghetti sandwich was clearly the only visitor in
Ivy's absence. Ivy suddenly felt very tired and
very small.

She went back out to the porch and lugged in
the heavy stacks of papers, to see if they contained any news of her parents' whereabouts.
They did not. However, Ivy did read a week's
worth of front page articles about the dastardly
kidnapping of Armilda and Borage Clott's most
beloved orphan (Will) by the cold-blooded and
obviously berserk and dangerous young desperado (herself).

"We loved that little boy with all our hearts,"
Borage Clott was quoted as saying ("in a voice
obviously choked with emotion," read the
Hollington Daily Times). His wife had taken to her
bed, too distraught to comment to the press.

And then Ivy read something that made her
smile.

The July 5 issue of *The Times* contained the
most interesting news that eleven-year-old Frank-
lin Rabidoux had won first prize in the 4th of

July Bicycle Decorating Contest. According to the article, Frank had ridden a bicycle that was festooned with empty Old Busthead Rye Whiskey bottles, and Commander Bimwhistle had fallen completely out of the judging stand in a dead faint. Before he hit the ground, his face had turned first red, then white, then purest, truest blue. The other assembled town officials had read this to be an impressive triple take of patriotic approval, and had awarded first prize to Frank in response. Ivy was especially pleased to note that nowhere in the article was there any mention of Frank Rabidoux having turned into a goat. The article concluded with the information that due to unusually severe thunderstorms, Frank's hot-air balloon ride had been postponed until the Hollington Bean Festival. And that, Ivy realized, was just a day away.

Ivy pushed aside the stack of newspapers and went out into her father's garden. Everything was terribly overgrown, of course, but apparently the unusual thunderstorm activity had kept the plants well watered. Ivy pulled a few weeds and wondered for the thousandth time what could have happened to her parents. Then she crossed to the far edge of the garden to see if Pearletta's collection of prizes had finally come tumbling down over the Greenes' lawn.

There stood the three outbuildings, bulging and brimming over as usual. But through the window of the last hut, Ivy saw something strange. It was just a movement, and a very small movement at that, and it was only strange because Ivy knew that months ago Pearletta had closed up that particular hut and had begun to store things in her new trailer.

Ivy simply had to know what was moving inside Pearletta's prize-packed storage hut. It could not be Pearletta, she knew, because it was still morning and that meant that Pearletta was pasted in front of her television set screaming, "I'd like to buy a vowel!" or, "Let's go for the bonus question, Wink!"

Ivy scrunched down low in Pearletta's overgrown grass and wriggled carefully (she was, after all, a most wanted, dangerous, and berserk desperado) to the end of the storage shed. She stretched her neck up ever so slowly, up and up, until she could just peer with one eye over the windowsill, and then she let out a shriek that would have awakened a ward full of African Sleeping Sickness victims had they been snoring nearby. For inside Pearletta's storage hut, sitting atop a fearsomely high stack of stereo equipment and yogurt makers, and looking pretty pleased about it, were her parents!

"Oh, my goodness!" said Ivy once she could speak.

Quickly she pried open the window and scrambled inside, knocking over a pile of authentic tortilla stuffers and a case of powdered hot dogs and not even caring about the noise she was making. Luckily, Pearletta's game shows were always the extremely loud kind, with lots of clapping and whooping, so that she was not likely to hear what was going on in her backyard.

Ivy's parents were every bit as delighted to see Ivy as she was to see them, although they were considerably less amazed.

"Why, Ivy, darling, how lovely you could drop in!" said her mother, after a round of hugs and kisses. "We've been wondering where you've been."

"Where *I've* been? Well, looking for you, of course! And in the Wretched Dear Darlings' Blessed Haven Orphanage, and in Cheese Bend with Aunt Zilpa, and, and, oh, never mind. *Where have you been!?!*"

"*Us?*" Ivy's mother and father said in bewildered unison. "Why, right here, of course. Care for a Tater Piffie?"

Ivy did not want a Tater Piffie, but from the

mounds of crumpled wrappers, it appeared that her parents had had quite a few.

Ivy's mother motioned to a sleek silver machine beside her.

"Would you like to wash your socks, dear? Oh, they come out lovely."

A ball of dread was gathering in Ivy's stomach. She looked down at her parents' feet. They were covered with gobs of sock mush.

"That's a juicer, Mom."

"A juicer! Now why on earth would anyone want to make sock juice?"

Ivy turned to her father. He was wearing a colander on his head and staring at a blank television set that lay upside-down in front of him.

"Dad, what are you doing?" Ivy asked, although she was pretty sure she would not like the answer.

"*Shhhhh!*" he replied. "It's time for the weather."

"But, Dad, the set's not on," said Ivy, now truly alarmed.

"Of course not," her father replied, in the voice you would use with someone who is very, very young or very, very dense. "It's *upside-down*, and *I'd lose my hat* if I tried to watch it."

Ivy did not have the courage to ask him why he

was wearing a colander. "Would you like me to turn the set right side up?"

There was a moment of profound silence as Ivy's father worked on this suggestion.

"What an extraordinary idea," he said finally, stunned. "Did you hear that, Velma? It's positively brilliant!"

Ivy sighed. Her parents were safe and in good health; apparently their diet of Tater Piffies and Zippa Cola had agreed with them, and for this, Ivy was truly grateful.

But they were dumber than soup.

Dusk fell. Just before she awakened Pierre for the trip back to Cheese Bend (the ostrich had stuffed himself into her father's golf bag and spent the day napping), Ivy made an anonymous phone call to her sister.

"Go over to 43 Popple Bottom Road and get your parents from the last storage shed. Bring them home with you and take extremely good care of them until you receive further notice. If you do not comply, my henchmen will plant your lawn with quack weed and dandelion, and paint your front door fuchsia." *Click.*

Ivy was beginning to enjoy being a dangerous and berserk desperado.

*   *   *

Ivy's next stop was the Wretched Dear Darlings' Blessed Haven Orphanage, where she wanted to do a little snooping around. She was surprised to see that the parlor lights were still on so late at night, and that a strange car stood in the driveway. The car was the extremely long and fancy kind, the expensive kind, that says very clearly, "*I'm* very important and *I've* got gobs of money and *you're* not worth a cupful of camel spit." On the side door, printed in gold letters, were the words Helmet-Hard Hair Spray Company. The words were somehow familiar to Ivy, but it took her a moment to realize why.

The newspapers. Somewhere in the stacks of newspapers that she had read that morning had been a short but interesting article about the Helmet-Hard Hair Spray Company and its battles with the Animals-Are-People-Too Crusaders. The animal rights group had maintained that the president of the Helmet-Hard Company loved nothing more than to slick down the fur of a few hundred puppies or kittens with hair spray, and then whack them senseless with baseball bats or light matches under their little paws or strap them to buses and send them careening off cliffs.

"Of course I love it!" the president had replied.

"I adore it, you bunch of meddling bunny-huggers! It's what scientific experimentation is all about!"

According to the article, the bunny-huggers had won, and Helmet-Hard was no longer allowed to test its products on animals. Ivy wondered what the president of the company could possibly have in common with Borage and Armilda Clott, except for the obvious fact that all three were perfectly rotten human beings. She maneuvered Pierre into the hedge below the parlor window to find out.

"So you can understand our little dilemma," said a man Ivy had never seen before, a man with a head as red as a boiled beet.

"Oh, perfectly; terrible nuisance the whole thing must be for you," agreed Armilda with a thoughtful nod of her wicked chin. "Now you'll have to perform your experiments on . . . something else."

"But I think we may be able to help," added Borage from the couch, taking his toes out of his mouth for a moment. "How many children were you looking for?"

"How many do you have?" asked the man with the boiled-beet head.

Chapter 12

Dumbstruck!

The next morning, back in Cheese Bend, bad news was dished up alongside the breakfast eggs. Ivy had just begun to relate the news of her trip to Zilpa and Will when Bubba and Dottie came up to the table. They were smiling, but their smiles were as brittle as new ice, and their cheeks were stained with tears.

"Oh, Will, we have the m-m-m-most w-w-w-wonderful news for you!" Dottie began, her lower lip trembling like Bubba's famous towering Jell-O mold. "You're being ad-d-d-dopted!"

"It was just on the news," continued Bubba, his eyes juicing up like Dottie's famous onion soup.

"The reporter called it the human interest story of the decade! Every child at the Wretched Dear Darlings' Blessed Haven Orphanage is being adopted next week by some fabulously wealthy couple from ... where did they say, Dottie, honey, was it Meadowmeade? Oh, well, they have a fleet of ponies and a pool the size of Lake Erie and a backyard carnival and trained monkey acts and a working volcano in the dining room and, and ... Anyway, Will, you know Dottie and I had been hoping we could adopt you after this runaway business was cleared up, but now it just wouldn't seem right to keep you from such a wonderful opportunity. We're so happy for you, and for all the others!"

Bubba did not look the slightest bit happy, nor did Dottie. Will looked as though he had just been told he was going to be fed to sharks.

"He's not going," said Ivy firmly, "and neither are the others."

Ivy and Zilpa hurriedly packed sleeping bags and five gallons of mint chocolate chip ice cream, and headed for the summit of Mount Roquefort for some serious problem solving, leaving Will in charge of Pierre. On the way, Ivy finished telling

her aunt what the Clotts were up to, and Zilpa
agreed that they would have to attend to the situation immediately.

"But we'll have to do it ourselves, Ivy. Chief
Firmstone thinks that the Clotts are angels of
kindness and you're a kidnapper!"

"We can do it. And we'd better figure out what
to do about my parents, too," Ivy said as she and
her aunt neared the top of the mountain. Up
they climbed, right through the clouds and into
the layer of air that acted as fertilizer on brains,
that grew ideas thick as weeds.

Ivy emerged first and was immediately struck
with an idea, blinding in its brilliance and stunning in its simplicity.

"That's it!" Ivy cried. "The answer, it's up
here!"

Zilpa popped up through the clouds in time to
hear Ivy's announcement.

"Of course, Ivy, I've always said we'd figure it
out up here."

"No, no, I mean *it's really up here;* we're standing in it, we're breathing it, we're smartening up
in it! Look, what is it my parents are missing?
Their common sense, right? They lost their wits,
their brain juice, or whatever you want to call it,
and I think *it's up here.* I think it's swirling around
up here in this, this *brain fog,* or whatever it is!"

Zilpa was silent for a moment as the new idea made itself at home in her head.

"It probably seeps out as you get older," she said, finally, nodding her head thoughtfully, "like earwax, or hair oil, little by little; and that's why children are so much smarter than adults!"

Zilpa had always maintained that this was true. "What do adults do all day?" she would ask, and then answer, "Work! And what do children do? Play! There you go! I rest my case!" As a result of this theory, she steadfastly refused to vote for anyone running for office who was over the age of twelve, and she encouraged all of her friends to follow the same practice.

"Why, if I hadn't lost so much of the stuff myself I'd have seen it, too, Ivy. But that still doesn't explain what happened to your parents. They lost it all at once, had it sucked right out of them like lemonade on an August day. They were *dumbstruck*, Ivy, that's exactly what they were, and we've got to figure out what triggered it."

Ivy and Aunt Zilpa spent the rest of the day eating ice cream and tossing about possible causes, ranging from alien invasions to mutant dandruff shampoo. Not surprisingly, Zilpa's favorite had to do with the moon.

"Remember, dear, you said there was no moon out that last night you heard your parents. That means there was a new moon, and the new moon is really the few days a month when the moon is seen thin and pale in the daytime sky, and invisible at night; pass me another bowl of mint chocolate chip, would you, honey? Why, that means it was just a month ago it happened, because tonight is the first night of the new moon. It's a loose and witchy time, a time when my skin doesn't seem nearly strong enough to hold me together."

But even she couldn't explain why millions of folks each month weren't dumbstruck, if being out under a new moon was all it took for people's senses to start heading north like migrating polar bears.

Finally they gave up for the night.

"Whatever it is, I sure wish it would happen to the Clotts," said Ivy, and then she and Aunt Zilpa nestled way down into their sleeping bags, pulling them well over their heads, as the air was a bit chilly at such a high altitude.

And it was a good thing they did this.

Chapter 13

Disaster's on the Menu

"Wake up, Ivy! Oh dearie me, oh merciful jelly beans! Disaster's on the menu at the Kozy Korner Kafe, and Pierre's the main ingredient! I've had the most brain-crackling dream, a real ripsnorter! It's only three o'clock in the morning, but we've got to head back right now."

Ivy poked her head out of her sleeping bag. "What was the dream?"

"It was all jumbled up, scrambled as eggs, but there was a purple onion, and the restaurant's flour sifter, and hello, hello, there was Pierre!"

Armed with flashlights, they picked their way down the mountain peak under a sky as black as rolling tar, a sky so black and thick it seemed to cling to their hair and creep up their nostrils.

"New moon, Ivy, remember? The darkest nights of the month, especially up here where there are no other lights."

Ivy had never seen it so perfectly dark before . . . except for the night that her parents disappeared.

Several hours later, when dawn first cracked the blackness, Ivy and Zilpa opened the door to the kitchen at the Kozy Korner Kafe to find things very badly out of whack indeed. Six inches of flour lay on the floor. Pierre had wedged himself into the lettuce basket of the restaurant-sized salad spinner and was whirling around at a speed that threatened to launch him into orbit, but no one else was around.

A dreadful crash came from inside the walk-in freezer (restaurants often have freezers the size of your living room). Ivy and Zilpa found Bubba sledding inside, his wig hanging off one ear like a single orange earmuff. He had heaped the entire stock of ice cream (and this was a colossal amount, as Bubba made it a practice to have a three-month supply of all thirty-seven flavors known to mankind on hand at all times) into one mountainous pile in the center, and was rocketing down this on a buttered restaurant tray. The fact that he always ended his run by crashing into the wall or a frozen side of beef did not seem to bother him at all.

Pierre managed to extricate himself from the salad spinner and came over to investigate.

"*Borkx!*" he cried, upon spying Bubba's gleaming, wigless, egg-shaped head. He seized the nearest nest-shaped thing he could find, a large silver bowl of leftover spaghetti, and planted it firmly upon Bubba's head. This seemed to please the large man greatly.

"Marvelous thinking!" he cried. "A crash helmet! Tallyho!"

"Wait, where's Dottie?" Ivy asked with sudden foreboding.

"Fishing," answered Bubba.

"Fishing where?"

"In the bathroom, of course. That's the only place here that's got a fishing hole!"

Ivy and Zilpa raced to the bathroom, with Pierre and Bubba hot on their tracks. There they found Dottie, bare feet firmly planted on the rim of the bathtub, casting into the water beneath her.

"No luck yet," she informed them, waving cheerfully.

"Dottie, please come down," Ivy urged.

"Can't," answered Dottie happily. "Glued my

feet to the rim so I wouldn't slip in anymore!" She beamed and motioned to the tube of Super Insta-Bond, quite proud of her cleverness.

Ivy remembered that Loel Hoober always carried a chain saw in the back of his truck for beard-trimming emergencies, and she ran out to fetch him at once.

The work was painstaking and delicate, but Loel was able at last to free Dottie from the tub, leaving her wearing a pair of porcelain soles. While Loel was occupied, Pierre tried to pack blue-dye toilet freshening tablets into the round tunnels of his beard, but Ivy wouldn't let him. She could just imagine the color his beard would turn after his next drink of water.

The little group trooped back to the kitchen after thanking Loel and waving good-bye to him. Just then Will came in, awakened no doubt by all the commotion. He stared at Dottie and Bubba.

"You're not ready," he said, clearly surprised.

"Of course we're ready," Dottie assured him. "Ready for what?"

"For breakfast," Will said slowly, as though he thought Dottie were playing a joke on him, but he just couldn't figure out what was funny.

"Breakfast! What a splendid idea, I'm starving! How about you, Bubba?"

"No, no, for your breakfast customers!"

"What on earth do you mean?" Bubba asked, scratching the large silver bowl he still wore on his head.

"The breakfast customers out there," Will said, leading Dottie to the swinging doors and opening them a crack.

"Bubba! The oddest thing! Mona and Mavis Grimble are out front sitting at a table, and lots of others, and now look, here comes that nice young man with the beard, Loel Hoober. Now where have I seen him before? They seem to be waiting for something. Whatever can it mean?"

Will looked very worried now. "They're here for their breakfast. They order it, and you cook it and serve it to them, and then they pay you for it. It's what running a restaurant is all about . . . it's your business!"

"Our *business!* It's *brilliant!* We make food and serve it and people *pay us* for it! Did you hear that, Dottie, the boy's a genius!" cried Bubba.

"Oh, Bubba, could it really work? Oh, let's try it! I'll go see if the Grimble cousins would like a meal."

But Ivy was quicker; she went out and wisely sent all the customers home. When she returned, Will ran up to her.

"Oh, Ivy, Bubba and Dottie are making snow angels in the flour! They've gone *completely looney,* but they were perfectly fine last night! I think it's like your parents."

Ivy thought so, too. "Think back, Will, did anything unusual happen last night?"

"Well, I heard something in the middle of the night; an explosion, I thought. It was too dark to see anything, but then I heard Bubba and Dottie outside. They were coughing, and then Bubba said, 'My wig!' and Dottie said, 'Are you pulling my hair?' and then they both started laughing, so I figured everything must be all right, and I went back to bed."

" 'Are you pulling my hair?' " Ivy repeated. "My mother said, 'Are you vacuuming my hair?' Will, do you know what time this was? It's very important!"

"I'm sorry, I don't."

"I do," said Aunt Zilpa, who had been examining the flour sifter. "I rigged up some of the appliances to timers, so Bubba wouldn't have to get up so early to start the day's baking. This machine here, for example, sifts all the flour by eleven thirty, and then sends it down the chute to the Batter King so that exactly at midnight the bread dough can be mixed. The bread dough in turn is then sent to the kneader, which then pops it into the rising pans. When Bubba comes down in the morning it's all ready for him to shape into whatever buns and loaves and rolls he'll need for the day. It's a marvelously clever system, if I do say so myself. But look here!" Zilpa pointed to a bulge in the stainless steel chute that led from the flour sifter to the Batter King.

"There's a Bermuda onion wedged up here, the same Bermuda onion, I'm afraid, that Pierre has been carrying around all week. He must have waited till everyone was asleep. Bag after fifty pound bag of fine white flour came pouring out of the flour sifter and shot down this chute, but couldn't get past this onion. Just before midnight there must have been a horrendous explosion. It would have awakened Bubba and Dottie, and they would have come running down to the kitchen to see what was wrong. There they would have found five hundred pounds of sifted flour hanging chokingly in the air, which probably sent them reeling out the back door, gasping and sputtering. That's when you heard them, Will; the Dobbelinas were outside exactly at midnight. *New moon* midnight! Will, did you notice anything else at all?"

"No, I couldn't see anything, it was perfectly dark."

There was utter silence as the same thought struck Ivy and Zilpa.

"It was perfectly *dark!*" cried Zilpa.

"It was *perfectly* dark!" cried Ivy. *"That's it! That's* what it takes to be Dumbstruck! It's like the night-blooming stenchweed, that only blooms when it's *perfectly* dark—the tiniest little scrap of light, and it just won't happen! Your brain juice can only come gushing out of your head in *total darkness*, and my dad says that's almost impossible to find these days. Perfect darkness only happens *exactly at midnight* on a night when there's no moon, and no other lights around; that's exactly how it was the night my parents were outside!"

"But, Ivy," Aunt Zilpa reminded her, "we were outside last night exactly at midnight in the perfect darkness, too, and it didn't happen to us."

"No, we weren't," Ivy replied after a moment's thought, "we were under our sleeping bags. Our *heads* were *covered!* And later, when we hiked back, it was three o'clock in the morning so it wasn't *perfectly* dark!"

And then Ivy had a thought.

"You said new moon lasts for a couple of nights, Aunt Zilpa. That means tonight is also new moon. Wouldn't it be a marvelous thing if Borage and Armilda Clott happened to wander outside at midnight tonight?"

"A perfectly wonderful thing, but you're forgetting the Bean Processing Plant next door to the orphanage. It lights up half of Hollington Valley."

Ivy smiled. "Oh, I'm not forgetting it at all. I think I have a plan."

Ivy got to work immediately. The first thing she did was compose a note to the Clotts:

Dear Clotts,

We are desperately anxious to buy your orphans. Our plans for these children are so cruel and despicable and painful that we cannot even mention them here, or tell you our names. But we are willing to pay one million dollars! Urgent you meet us *outside, in your courtyard, at exactly midnight!*

P.S. DO NOT WEAR HATS!!!

Ivy sealed the envelope and marked it Special Hand Delivery. Just then Zilpa came into the room.

"That was Myrtle's new husband, Oswell, on the phone. The strangest thing . . ."

"Does he know I'm here?" Ivy interrupted, worried.

"No, but he does know that you glued an eyeball onto Myrtle's forehead on the day of last year's Bean Festival Beauty Pageant. He kept asking me everything about it—how you did it, how long she was conked out."

"Why would he want to know all that?"

"Seems your sister's a finalist in this year's pageant," Zilpa said, trying not to smile. "Today's the Bean Festival, and Oswell was wondering if he could borrow an eyeball before she wakes up!"

"There may be some hope for him after all," said Ivy. "Call him back and tell him this: He can go over to my house right now and get one from my jewelry box, but he's got to promise to have my parents on the roof of his house by noon today. Oh, and one more thing. The gas venting pipe at the Bean Processing Plant; ask him how big around it is."

Then Ivy called her old friend Frank Rabidoux. When he heard Ivy's predicament and her plan, he promised at once to help.

"Oh, and one more thing, Frank. The gumwad ball; how big around is it now?"

Chapter 14

"Up, Up, and Away"

Ivy and Zilpa took the early train, and arrived in Hollington well before noon. They wore hats with the brims pulled way down like all good desperadoes do, and joined the happy throngs of Festival-goers heading for the airfield without being recognized. On the way, they stopped at the Wretched Dear Darlings' Blessed Haven Orphanage. Ivy laid her note on the doorstep, rang the bell, and then hid in the hedge below the parlor window with Aunt Zilpa.

Armilda and Borage Clott picked up the mysterious note and read it right on the doorstep.

"Well, well, well," mused Armilda. "It doesn't

rain but it pours. Now we have *two* offers to buy our disgusting orphans, and, strangely enough, the Helmet-Hard Company also offered a million dollars."

"It seems a shame to have to give up one million dollar payment to get the other," said Borage greedily.

"No reason that we have to," Armilda answered him, "if we are clever about it. Come inside; I have an idea." Then Ivy heard Armilda settle herself at the desk in the parlor. Ivy raised herself up just enough to peek through the window.

Presently, Armilda handed Borage a piece of paper. "Read this note I'm sending over to the Helmet-Hard people."

Borage read the note aloud:

Urgent you meet us tonight in our courtyard at exactly fifteen minutes past midnight! Bring the one million smackers! You may collect the "goods" tomorrow morning if all is in order.

P.S. DO NOT WEAR HATS!!!

Borage sucked his toes for awhile as he pondered the note Armilda had written.

"Why the bit about the hats?" he asked his bony wife.

"I don't know. But I liked the sound of it in the other note," she answered her lumpy husband.

"Of course, when the Helmet-Hard people come to collect the little weasels in the morning, they're going to be awfully disappointed to find them already gone."

"Most likely they'll be furious," Armilda agreed, with a wicked grin. "Beside themselves with rage, probably; popping their corks. But, as we'll be off on a cruise around the world with two million smackers in our pockets, I don't think we're going to worry about it too much!"

Borage laughed so hard he nearly bit off a toe.

There is nothing like a Bean Festival to bring out the joy of living in a town, and this year's event was no exception. Merrymakers crowded the Better Living Through Beans exhibition, and a great many folks were enjoying a lively game of Bean Bingo. But most of the townspeople were drifting toward the hot-air balloon launching pad where preparations were already underway for Frank Rabidoux's lift-off.

The Hollington Glee Club finished a rendition of "We Are the Beans" with more enthusiasm than talent. Then they lurched gamely into "Up, Up, and Away," which was the signal for Commander Bimwhistle to climb to the podium and begin the launching ceremony.

Ivy and Zilpa edged nearer to the launching pad, where they caught Frank's eye and signaled. Frank climbed into the balloon carrying a box the size of a birthday cake, and waved to the crowd. The crowd, carefree in the frenzied flush of Festival fever, showered the balloon with good wishes and beans; lots of beans. There were broad beans, butter beans, Italian flats and pintos, waxed beans, stringless greens, scarlet runners, and limas; and in the celebration, no one noticed Ivy and her aunt making their way up to the basket.

The tether cutting began, and soon the balloon was attached to the earth by only one line. The pilot turned to shake hands with Commander Bimwhistle before hopping aboard. And then, at the last possible moment, Frank Rabidoux leaped out of the basket, and Ivy and Zilpa leaped in and cut the line.

The balloon surged up majestically on the freshening breeze, completely ignoring the pilot who was hopping up and down on the launching pad, shaking his fist and shouting, "Come back down this instant!" In only a few moments, Zilpa had figured out the controls on the burner (it is really quite simple, any fool at all could do it: more heat to rise, less to come down) and was heading toward Ivy's first destination.

Liberty Acres loomed ahead like a game-board neighborhood; flat-lawned and treeless. Its houses were identical cubes, and it would have been impossible to tell which one was Myrtle's except that there were two people perched on top of it. Zilpa swooped down and lowered the rope.

"Climb aboard!" she called to Ivy's parents.

This they managed to do, but once aboard it was immediately apparent that Ivy's mother and father still had less sense than God gives to pumpkins.

"Oh, I've forgotten my paintbrush!" Ivy's mother chirped. "I'll just pop out and get it!"

And she hopped over the rim and stepped out into thin air. Luckily, her foot was entangled in one of the lines, and Zilpa and Ivy were able to haul her back in like a net full of codfish.

Ivy's father was busy trying to compose a poem, but trying to compose a poem without brains is like trying to make ice without water.

> *Hooray, we're in a balloon,*
> *Never eat your baboon,*
> *Tomorrow is yesterday soon,*
> *Your mother is quite a raccoon!*

Zilpa and Ivy looked at each other. "Let's hope this works," they said at the same instant.

Zilpa cranked up the flame and they shot straight up like a rocket toward the layer of brain fog hanging above the clouds that Ivy prayed might soak back into her parents' pitifully empty heads.

"Go up as high as you can," Ivy urged her aunt. "Higher than the monks in Tibet!"

Ivy and Zilpa kept their hats pulled firmly around their heads as neither of them was willing to find out what might happen to a reasonably full brain in the mysterious layer of smart stuff. Ivy had asked Zilpa to line their hats with aluminum foil as an added precaution.

As soon as they reached the upper stratosphere, higher up, even, than Mount Roquefort, Ivy saw her parents regain their wits. The haze cleared from their fuddled eyes, and a dawn broke dazzlingly.

"Oh!" said Ivy's father.

"Oh!" said Ivy's mother.

Both of them seemed to realize for the first time that they were in a balloon far above the earth, and they began to discuss air pressure and velocity and wind currents with a refreshing intelligence. Ivy filled them in on what had happened, while Zilpa guided the balloon through

the afternoon sky toward majestic Mount Roquefort for the next rendezvous.

"I can't risk landing this thing, as we may not
get off again," she said, as the Cheese Bend town
square came into view. "There's the maple tree
where Pierre and Will are supposed to be waiting; oh, yes, I see them now! Boyd and Velma,
you make yourself at home at my place and keep
a watch over Dottie and Bubba until I get back.
I'll swing low over the duck pond so you can
jump out."

Ivy's parents dove out, and in just a minute,
they bobbed to the surface of the pond and
waved the balloon good-bye. Zilpa maneuvered
the basket to the top of the maple tree where Will
and Pierre were perched, and the two of them
hopped aboard. And then the branches parted
and a third passenger jumped in . . . Florinda!

"I've looked on a map," she cried, her enor-
mous lips flapping like rubber sausages, "and
Hollington is closer to Hollywood than Cheese
Bend is. I'm coming with you!"

"Very well," said Aunt Zilpa, adjusting the
flame for the balloon to rise higher, "but take
care not to open your mouth too suddenly, or
you'll disturb the air flow."

Florinda promised to be careful, and the group
took off into the gathering blue of evening. They

made good time back to Hollington, and dropped Florinda off on top of Pearletta Swicegood's storage trailer at Ivy's suggestion.

"Just knock on her door and introduce yourself. I have a feeling you two are going to hit it off."

Night fell and deepened. The hot-air balloon hung motionless in the moonless sky above the Hollington Bean Processing Plant. The plant sprawled like a sleeping dragon a hundred yards below, emitting a sickly green light across the town. The glow was especially bright on the Wretched Dear Darlings' Blessed Haven Orphanage next door, and Ivy could make out Borage and Armilda Clott whispering together in the courtyard. They were not wearing hats.

Ivy looked at her watch: fifteen minutes to midnight. Just then, a car pulled into the orphanage driveway. A very long and fancy car, and Ivy knew whose it was even though she could not read the gold lettering on its side.

The president of the Helmet-Hard Hair Spray Company got out, followed by a little man who trotted behind him meekly. The little man carried a sack that appeared to be very heavy, and was just about the right size, Ivy thought, to hold one million dollars. Neither man was wearing a hat.

"But, sir," the little man's voice drifted up, "the note says fifteen minutes *past* midnight."

"Exactly," said the president, nodding his boiled-beet head at the note he had just pulled out of his pocket. "But something smells fishy here."

"Very fishy indeed," agreed the little man, sniffing the note.

"It's the fifteen minutes past midnight part; so we're going to arrive in that courtyard a bit early and have ourselves a little look-see around. No one's going to pull a fast one on the president of the Helmet-Hard Hair Spray Company!"

And then the two of them crept around to the back entrance of the courtyard, chuckling quietly.

Zilpa lowered the balloon a little bit. "I can't get too near the Bean Processing Plant, you know. The gas coming out of that pipe could blow us to smithereens. This is as close as I dare to come."

"It'll have to be close enough," said Ivy, glancing at her watch again. "It's time. Will, wake Pierre."

Ivy pulled out the box that Frank Rabidoux had left under the seat and opened it up. The large ball inside smelled of peppermint and cinnamon and juicy fruit and old spit, and Ivy thought fondly of the good times she and Frank had spent together, with their collecting scrapers in hand.

"Farewell," she said, saluting. "Go in glory."

And then she showed the gum-wad ball to Pierre.

Pierre came to full alert status at once, every feather trembling in his excitement. Ivy led him to the side of the basket and pointed to the circle of light that was the gas venting pipe. And that was all she had to do.

Pierre seemed to know exactly what was needed, and he rose to the task magnificently. Where stuffing round things into round places was concerned he was a true professional, an artist and athlete combined, a thing of splendid beauty and graceful perfection. The ostrich lifted the gum-wad ball and held it a moment, judging its density and weight. He eyed the pipe below for distance and dimension. And then he fired. *"BORKX!"*

The gum-wad ball sailed into the embrace of the waiting bean gas venting pipe. You'd have sworn the things were magnetized.

"Let's get out of the way," shouted Ivy. "She may blow at any minute!"

Zilpa made a gentle landing in front of the

orphanage. She and Ivy quickly deflated the balloon and set it up, tentlike around them all, and then settled down to watch.

Almost immediately the Bean Processing Plant began to rumble and groan. It began to shake and rattle fearfully. And then, from its pipe, it began to blow a bubble. The bubble grew at an astonishing rate, filled from the tremendous pressure of the vented bean gas, until it reached the size of a circus tent. Still it did not pop, for it had been cured over the years to the toughness of space-age plastic. Larger and larger still it grew, that enormous bubble, until finally, at one minute till midnight, it could hold no more. The bubble blew wide open with a tremendous *whooooosh*, settling its sticky skin over every square inch of the Hollington Bean Processing Plant.

And covering every light.

"Quick," Ivy said, "turn on the flashlight, Will, so we're not in the dark at midnight. But take care not to let any light shine out. And hang on to Pierre!"

At exactly midnight, it was perfectly, totally, and completely dark in the miserable orphanage courtyard where the four nasty people were planning their nasty plans. As easily as water is wrung out of a sponge, the juice of their thoughts, of their very ability to think, was wrung out of their brains. At that precise instant three of them felt a slight tugging at their hair and one of them felt a slight tugging on his lumpy and grayish bald scalp. All four of them began to giggle as every last drop of their wits went soaring free into the pitch-black sky.

Chapter 15

"Open Your Mouth, Armilda"

What a celebration it was at the Wretched Dear Darlings' Blessed Haven Orphanage. Will threw open the kitchen and cooked the orphans delicacies remarkable enough to make French chefs weep with envy. There was merrymaking of every sort you could imagine, and even some merrymaking you might not imagine if you happen to be the quiet type. It was such a celebration that even when those orphans were doddering old grandfathers and grandmothers they would still call each other up and say, "Do you remember the night that Ivy Greene took care of the Clotts? Now that," they would remind themselves, "was a celebration."

And later, when they were all too tired to celebrate for even one second longer, they each chose their favorite room from the fifty that Borage and Armilda had been keeping to themselves and went to sleep. On pillows!

The Helmet-Hard people had scampered off into the night after dropping their heavy sack in the courtyard and were never heard of again. Borage and Armilda, however, wandered inside the orphanage.

"Hello, Clotts," said Ivy, when she spotted the pair walking aimlessly around in the parlor. "You must be looking for some work to do."

"Oh, yes!" they both cried eagerly, greatly pleased to latch on to any idea at all.

"Will, what do you think the Clotts ought to do first? Laundry? The dishes, perhaps? Clean the bathrooms, or scrape out the chimneys?"

"No," said Will thoughtfully, "I believe the Clotts would like to get rid of the spiders."

Borage and Armilda looked at the thousands upon thousands upon thousands of spiders on the ceiling. Borage reached up to gather a handful.

"But where should we put them?"

"I haven't the faintest idea."

"Wait! Open your mouth again, Armilda!"
She did, and Borage filled it up with spiders.
"There! All gone! Now you try, Armilda." And
he opened his mouth and his wife crammed a
handful in.
"*Mmmmm, crunchy!*" said Borage.
"Delicious," agreed Armilda.

Florinda Van der Vonne dropped by the orphanage the next day with her new friend Pearletta
Swicegood.

"Please come in," said Ivy, who had had a nice
long sleep, an excellent breakfast, and an idea.
"Let me show you around all the lovely *large*
rooms here; large enough for, oh, say, keeping
lots of prizes, Pearletta. Perhaps we could all
watch a game show. Florinda, could you hostess it
for us?"

Pearletta and Florinda never left. For in the
orphanage Pearletta found what she had never
found before in her entire life: a place where she
was needed. Pearletta, who did not have a mean
bone in her body (only several foolish ones),
found that she was needed to read children stories and to see that their teeth were brushed and
that they had fresh socks every day and a hundred other things. She never gave up her game

shows, and Florinda seemed to find a deep and true happiness in hostessing them for her. Pearletta also discovered that she did quite well playing children's game shows as well, and the orphans were delighted with all the marvelous prizes she won and felt that they had everything in life that they could ever need. The million dollars found lying around in the courtyard went a long way toward seeing that this was true.

Borage and Armilda were allowed to stay at the orphanage, and they were trained to perform the simpler jobs that had to do with cleaning, such as sweeping and washing and scrubbing. (My friends, cleaning is mindless work, and quite possibly harmful to your health, and I strongly advise you to avoid it at any cost.) In fairness, the orphans dressed the Clotts up every Sunday and took them out for a lovely walk across the park, and let them have those enormous glass lollipops, which Borage and Armilda enjoyed very much. But, then, you must remember, they were as dumb as dirt.

Will stayed on at the Wretched Dear Darlings' Blessed Haven Orphanage for awhile, setting up a proper kitchen and teaching his friends the best of Bubba and Dottie's recipes, while Zilpa took the Dobbelinas up to the very top of Mount Roquefort to camp out in the brain fog until they recovered their wits. Then, of course, the little boy went back to Cheese Bend where he belonged all along.

Ivy stayed on at the orphanage for a few days, too, just to see that everything was running smoothly, but the very instant she could, she ran straight home. Her parents were there, and they were fine, and that was the best gift she could have gotten. But there was something else as well.

After her trips to the top of Mount Roquefort with Aunt Zilpa, Ivy was undeniably smarter. In fact, it was soon apparent that Boyd and Velma's younger daughter was positively brilliant, an *absolute genius,* who had only, for example, to glance at the thickest textbook to understand it completely. After only a few days of classes that fall, even the dullest of her teachers had to admit that there was nothing more that they could teach her, and so she was excused from school for the rest of her life.

Which suited Ivy perfectly.